MURDER AMONG THE HIVES

MILLER'S MAGICAL MYSTERIES

BOOK ONE

ELOISE EVERHART

ALORIUM PUBLISHING

PB ISBN: 978-1-962759-09-0

Author: Eloise Everhart

Editors: Rashida Breen and Sarah Carleton

Cover design by GetCovers

CHAPTER 1

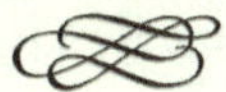

I craned my neck and stared up at City Hall, a three-story brick building that loomed over the street. I tried not to twitch as cars sped behind me. Being surrounded by so many people was new.

For the past twenty-five years, ever since my witch powers had arrived in my senior year of high school, I'd spent almost every waking minute on my farm. Until recently, the citizens of Point Pleasant, Washington, hadn't wanted me around. A nasty side effect of a curse my grandmother had been struck with was that every witch in her family, once they came into their powers, was distrusted on sight. I'd been a pariah around town until the curse was broken eight months ago. The distrust had been even worse when I'd visited Seattle. At least here on Whidbey Island, the people had been too nice to do much more than glower, whisper, engage in the occasional prank, or throw eggs at my house. In Seattle, a security guard had chased me down the street after I made the mistake of stopping outside a boutique store.

I squared my shoulders and held my head up high, a trick my mother had taught me when I was young. People felt more uncomfortable going after someone who looked confident. To show weakness was to invite an attack. For years, always smiling and always keeping my head up was the best defense I had.

My mouth went dry, and the palms of my hands began to sweat as I strode toward the front doors. *It's just a job. If they didn't want me here, they wouldn't have hired me, right?*

The front doors opened into a large foyer with a receptionist desk along the back wall. *Desk* was probably the wrong term for the massive piece of furniture that ran almost the entire length of the room. I studied it as I moved closer. The thing looked like it was original to the building. It was constructed out of a single piece of wood that must have come from an old-growth forest. There were no seams anywhere. The wood was so smooth it shone under the lights. Seated behind it, small by comparison, was a woman who looked only a few years younger than me. She was in her late thirties, with hair swept back into a loose French twist and a navy-blue blazer over a cream blouse. Her eyes were lined with a dark plum that made their green pop.

"Megan Miller?" The receptionist smiled tightly as I approached.

"That's me." I held my arms motionless at my sides and straightened farther, tilting my head to give myself a haughty expression. *I won't let her see my nerves. I was asked to be here.*

"Excellent." She slid a badge across the table toward me. The photo I had sent them was printed on the front, with the words *Point Pleasant City Employee* stamped across the top.

The ID card didn't list my position. I wasn't sure what they were calling me anyway. I would be a liaison between the city council and the Wardens of the West, a group that was effectively the national police force for the supernatural community. The masses didn't know about the presence of witches or other supernatural beings. I would probably be listed as some sort of consultant. Or a probationary consultant. I needed to make it through my trial period first before I got the job permanently.

I gave the receptionist an equally tight smile as I clipped the ID card to my chest.

"The council is already in session." The woman cocked her head toward a hallway on her left. "You should head on back. They're expecting you."

"Thank you." I forced the words out of my mouth, which had somehow managed to get even dryer since I'd walked into the building.

I smoothed my hands down my pants legs and strode down the hallway, my mind going a mile a minute. The new job had been sprung on me unexpectedly only three days before, at a wedding. A member of my coven, Dani, had married the local sheriff after a whirlwind romance. Somehow, at the end of the reception, I'd been roped into a new job. Not that I needed one—I had my farm—but *Never say no to the Wardens* was like the fifth unspoken rule of the magical community. I had a feeling that messing it up during my trial period would be just as bad as if I had said no. The Wardens didn't strike me as being the forgiving type.

I peered down at my outfit as I hovered outside the council meeting-room doors. Until recently, my entire wardrobe had been made up of jeans, tank tops, and flannel. My coven had taken me shopping for work clothes, and I'd foolishly stopped them at three pairs of black slacks and a few wrap shirts. The receptionist looked so much more fashionable in comparison. *Should I have bought a skirt? Oh god. I'm still wearing work boots. Will anyone take me seriously here?*

I shook my head and reached for the door. My fingers froze around the handle as voices rose in anger on the other side. The wood was thick enough that I couldn't make out what was being said. *Is it about me? Am I really that late? I got here exactly on time. What if they're like my dad was and anything short of fifteen minutes early is late?* I clenched my fist around the knob and steadied my breathing. Then I turned the handle and pushed the door inward.

The council meeting room was larger than I'd expected. It reminded me of a court room. Along the back wall was a long table with a few people sitting behind it. My gaze bounced from face to face. I recognized the city councilors from the town's website, which I had perused the night before. I mentally put names to faces. On the far left was Edgar Graves. He had a strong, prominent jaw that was jutted forward in a scowl and wore a tan suit with a brown tie. Next to him was Helen Stokes. Her graying hair was pulled into a tight bun at the base of her neck. She wore a pastel-blue cardigan over a floral blouse. Between them and the other two city council members stood Steven Bishop, the mayor, wearing a navy-blue suit, and a white shirt with the top button undone. His red tie was loosened a notch. His usually warm smile had been replaced with a tired expression. He swept his hands over his hair, which was short cropped and cut into a clean fade along the sides. My gaze continued down the line to the last two city councilors. Nicholas Reyes, the youngest and newest of the councilors, was leaning back in his seat. He looked almost out of place in a T-shirt and gray blazer. The last man at the table was Arthur Miles, the longest-serving councilman. His hair was almost completely white. He fiddled with a pocket watch as the room exploded into more arguing.

Facing off against the councilors was Miranda Blackwood. She stood on the left side of the room, separated from them by a wooden bar. She was the local warden of the west. Being this close to her terrified me. In the supernatural community, the Wardens frequently acted as judge, jury, and executioner when they felt one of their laws had been broken. The fact that she was stationed in town was disconcerting. And her insistence that I accept a liaison role between her and the town council had given me nightmares for the past two nights. The bad dreams had varied from the ridiculous—showing up to work on my first day naked—to the horrifying, such as this all turning out to be a test which culminated in Miranda Blackwood arresting me for... something.

Miranda slammed her hand against the bar. "Avery's death falls under my jurisdiction. This isn't up for debate. Her body needs to be handed over to me immediately."

My eyes widened. *What on earth is going on?*

"It's a murder in town," Sheriff Chris Harris cut in. He was on the right side of the room, leaning against the bar, his head half turned toward Miranda as he projected his voice to the councilors at the back of the room. "If the warden—"

I scurried into the room. Everyone there had been informed that supernaturals existed, but I somehow doubted the whole building knew. A door opened farther down the hall, changing the air pressure as I pushed the door to the council room closed. It jerked out of my hands and slammed shut. I winced as the entire room turned to stare at me. I wet my lips.

"Sorry." I stepped back from the door and gestured awkwardly to a chair along the back wall. "I'll, uh... I'll just wait over here."

Chris cleared his throat and shifted his focus back to Miranda and the councilors. "If the warden has information that could lead to an arrest, she should provide it. To my knowledge, the state of Washington doesn't recognize the Wardens of the West as a legitimate law enforcement agency. Avery was murdered. That's a crime, and therefore, it belongs on my desk."

Miranda scoffed. "Per the agreement the town and the Wardens reached, all supernatural issues are under my purview. This is a supernatural issue."

"Miranda." Steven shook his head. "That is not the exact

verbiage of the agreement, and you know it. Do you have any proof that this should be on your desk alone?"

My head swiveled back and forth as I tracked the verbal sparring matching. *What agreement? Is that why I'm here?* I gripped the edge of my seat as I inched forward. I had heard rumors that the town council was working with the Wardens on issues, but I didn't know a formal agreement had been reached.

Miranda scoffed again and drew herself up straight. She looked imperious in her deep-purple robes, with her jet-black hair streaming down her back. "I don't have to justify what is or isn't my jurisdiction. I am the expert when it comes to supernatural matters. If I have to slow down and explain everything to you all, investigations into *crimes* like this will get bogged down and killers will walk loose. My word should be taken. This is my jurisdiction."

Chris shook his head. "We're not toddlers. Taking a few minutes of your time to explain isn't that difficult. If she can't share a single reason why the case should be taken away from me, then it should stay where it belongs—on my desk."

Steven pinched the bridge of his nose. "We're talking in circles. Are there any further arguments we should hear before the council votes on the issue?"

"Votes?" Miranda slammed her hand down on the banister again. "It's my jurisdiction. There shouldn't be a vote. As… as nonmagical individuals, you can't possibly understand all the ins and outs of supernatural affairs. And if something were to come out during the sheriff's investigation that reveals our presence to the populace, what do you expect him to do to cover that up? He can't modify memories like some of my associates can. Don't do this."

Steven shot her a look of disbelief before he straightened his tie and turned his head to the left. "I'll take that as a no on any new arguments. Let's move on to the vote, then, shall we? Edgar, how do you vote on this issue?"

Edgar pushed his glasses farther up his nose. "No. The case stays with Sheriff Harris."

Steven nodded. "Helen?"

Helen fidgeted with the sleeves of her cardigan. "I've always believed in trusting the experts. In this case, Miranda is that expert. My vote is yes, it should be on her desk."

Steven turned to the right. "Nicholas?"

Nicholas tapped his fingers against the table and pursed his lips. "Yes, with a few caveats. Miranda should report her findings to us. I'm willing to extend trust, but she needs to show us she earned it before I'm willing to extend it again down the line. Plus, I think she should need to run this changing-memories thing by us before carting our constituents off to one of her coworkers."

Miranda crossed her arms and grumbled, "Fine."

My eyes flicked between her and the last council member, Arthur, who was still fiddling with his pocket watch. He didn't even look up as Steven said his name. Instead he pushed the watch into his waist pocket and blinked as he stared out the windows to his right.

"No," Arthur said.

Miranda spluttered.

Arthur cleared his throat. "Historically, crimes have been investigated and solved by the local sheriff's office. It has worked since our founding. If it isn't broken, why fix it?"

Steven leaned forward against the table. "I never thought I would miss Peter. I dislike having to cast the tiebreaker vote. The special election to fill his seat can't come soon enough."

"Well?" Miranda inched forward. "What will it be?"

"Give me a moment to think." Steven slumped into his seat and steepled his hands in front of his face.

I peered at him as his eyes flicked back and forth between the two options. On the one hand, he had Miranda, who fit the very definition of a prickly person but was the magical expert and could contain any information leaks about the supernatural community. On the other hand, he had Chris, a new sheriff with a spotless track record when it came to bringing people to justice but, though married to a witch, didn't have the same knowledge base as Miranda.

I didn't envy Steven's decision. As he contemplated, my mind whirled through the options. The pros and cons to both sides were equal. Miranda hadn't exactly proven herself trustworthy yet. *If only there were a third option.*

I sat up straight in my seat. There was a third option. Chris's wife, Dani, had helped him solve multiple cases involving supernatural elements. She could do it. And if she needed assistance with the containment side, she had an entire coven to help.

"What if there were another way?" I asked.

Every eye in the room turned toward me. The hair on the back of my neck rose, and I fought the urge to flee. After decades of such stares leading to insults and derision, it was hard to maintain my confident facade. My mother had trained me to stay out of the limelight. Holding my body still, I lifted my head.

I forced myself to appear calm and confident as I met each one of their gazes in turn. "There is another option. If I may present it?"

Steven motioned me forward.

I stood and walked to the center of the room, between Miranda and Chris, with my head held high. "Councilman Miles was mistaken when he implied only the sheriff's office has investigated and solved crimes. Dani Will—Dani Harris—has assisted in multiple investigations and—"

"Absolutely not." Miranda shook her head and pushed forward a step. She leaned over the banister that separated her from the council members. "If you expect the sheriff's wife to make an impartial decision on whether this should be on her husband's desk or mine, then you are delusional."

Next to me, Chris scoffed. It was almost laughable,

thinking Dani couldn't be impartial. My amusement bubbled up, and I covered my mouth before it could escape.

Miranda spun and glared at me. Every eye in the room was focused on my face. I forced my expression to remain neutral even as my heart pounded wildly. *Did I really just laugh?* My gaze bounced from face to face. They didn't know Dani like I did. *What can I say so I don't look stupid or overly defensive?*

I cleared my throat. "I was using Dani as an example. But... what about me? I am the liaison after all. I could investigate the case and figure out whose desk it actually belongs on."

Edgar raised an eyebrow. "You?"

Smiling at them and forcing my muscles to relax, I inched forward so that they were closer to me. My specialty was enchantment magic—when people were physically near me, they tended to like me. It wasn't effective one hundred percent of the time, but ever since the curse had been lifted, my specialty had made life easier. Despite that, it was hard not to flinch as everyone in the room tracked my movements.

My mouth was so dry. Too dry. It was hard to continue speaking as my voice became raspier. "Plus, I can contain things. I have some memory-altering powers of my own. I wouldn't need to send anyone off to an associate. I could handle it myself."

Steven smiled. It was a genuine smile that reached his eyes. He nodded and spread his hands out wide. "It looks like a third option has been put on the table. Does anyone want to officially add it?"

Helen raised her hand. "I put forth the motion to have Megan Miller investigate the case."

"Seconded," Arthur said.

"Excellent. Do we need time to debate?" Steven looked up

and down the table. All of the councilors shook their heads. "Then let's put this to a vote. Edgar?"

One by one, each of the councilors voted in my favor. As Arthur said the final yes, my heart skipped a beat. The investigation was mine.

What on earth am I supposed to do now? I opened and closed my mouth, unsure of what to say.

Steven shot me a relieved smile. "Excellent. You have your first assignment as the liaison—find the killer so we know who can make the arrest. If this goes well, you should be out of the probationary period in no time."

Chris eased toward me and patted me on the shoulder. "You're going to do great. Victor is retrieving the body from the apiary right now. He should be back in town in about an hour. Talking to him about his findings is probably a good place to start."

My shoulders slid down as the weight of the first decision was lifted off me. "Thanks." I took a step back toward the door. "Well, I... I should probably get started on that, then."

"Good luck, Miss Miller." Steven leaned back in his seat. "Welcome to the team. This should make a memorable first day for you. I look forward to hearing about what you discover after you've looked into things further. Now, let's move onto the next item of business. Abigail and Willow have finished the expansion of the Slice of Life diner. They want to have a grand-reopening event and have asked for some assistance with traffic control."

I backed out of the room and closed the door, cutting off the rest of their conversation, then forced myself to walk calmly down the hallway and out to my truck. Once I was safely behind the wheel, I pulled out my phone, my hands shaking from the stress of volunteering to lead a murder investigation, and typed out a message to my coven.

SOS. Emergency coven meeting needed ASAP.

Kim:
The Bizzy Bean?

Dani:
I'm already in the neighborhood.

Heather:
I already have a plate of cookies and coffees on standby.

Already? How did you know I would need your help so quickly?

Heather:
It's your first day. I had planned on them being celebratory, but emergency works too. What's wrong?

I'll tell you when I get there. It's a lot.

I shoved my phone into my pocket. I'd never investigated a crime before. Dani had, and I had lent her a hand on occasion, but this was the first time something this big had been on my shoulders.

Why couldn't I have kept my mouth shut? I'm a farmer, not a detective. I drove straight to my coven. They would know what to do. I needed all the advice I could get before I fell flat on my face in front of all those witnesses.

CHAPTER 2

I found a parking space outside the Bizzy Bean. Before heading inside, I paused to appreciate the new window art. Heather, the owner of the Bizzy Bean, changed it out once a month. Ever since she had changed the café's theme from bees to cats, the artwork had shifted. It was late spring, so the painting that covered the windows was of a white cat with a caramel star on her chest, romping through a field of flowers with bees trailing after her. Star, Heather's rescue kitty, was a frequent model for the art. She was also the only permanent cat resident and acted as a foster mother to all the kittens that went through her doors.

I stared at the painting, a small smile spreading across my lips. Heather, the only non-witch member of my coven, brought something to the table that none of the other women could—calm. I loved Dani and Kim, but Heather was our rock.

I pushed the front doors open and instinctively squared my shoulders and held my head high as the cacophony of voices hit me. Training my gaze on the booth in the back, where my coven was waiting for me, I strode through the swinging plexiglass doors into the cat enclosure. Kittens scampered around my legs as I moved through the room. I took in the scene through my peripheral vision. Another trick my mother had taught me was to always be aware of your surroundings. It was harder for people to sucker punch you if you saw the blow coming. For eight months, no hits had come my way, but awareness was a hard habit to break. I searched the faces of the customers for hostility. None of them looked my way.

Heather stood as I arrived and pulled me into a hug. "Even if your day is starting out rough, I still wanted to say congratulations. It's nice seeing you getting more involved in the community."

I squeezed her back and took my seat. I held my hands under the table. It was one I had built myself, designed to fit a large group of women. The top was made of resin embedded with crystals and flowers useful for protection spells. Around the table, sunken into the wood of the floor, was a braid of gold, silver, and iron, and at each of the corners, hidden under wooden panels, were mercury thermometers. This table was the safest place in all of Point Pleasant.

Heather shoved a plate of cookies to the center of the table and sat down opposite me. Kim and Dani both reached for one. Heather had made white-chocolate-strawberry macarons. My mouth watered. I grabbed one off the plate and nibbled at the corners as my coven members studied me.

Kim cleared her throat. "All right. You're one hour into your new job, and there's already an emergency. Who do I need to glower at for making your day difficult?"

Dani nodded. "With Grace being in her twenties, I'm a bit out of practice, but I'm more than willing to throw my best mom voice into the mix."

"I've got a killer disappointed look," Heather chimed in. "Who's on the naughty list?"

I half covered my face with my hands. "Me."

Heather snorted and threw a hand over her mouth in a desperate attempt to smother a laugh.

"Okay…?" Kim said, dragging out the word until it rose at the end like a question.

I sagged in my seat. "I made a dumb decision, and I need your help figuring out how to get out of it, or at the very least not fall flat on my face in front of my new boss."

"What happened?" Dani asked.

I grimaced. "I may have impulsively volunteered to investigate a murder."

"Oh…" Dani relaxed into her seat. "Well, that's not too bad. My schedule's flexible. I'll help."

I peered at Dani through my fingers. "I'm not sure that's a good idea."

Dani's jaw slackened as she stared at me. She opened and closed her mouth as if searching for the right words.

Oh god. She thinks I don't want her help. Have I hurt her feelings? I'm so bad at this being-a-friend thing. Abort. Abort.

I grabbed her hand. "I volunteered because Chris and Miranda were butting heads over it. I wouldn't want to put you in hot water with either one. As much as I would love you going out there with me, I think it would be best if I handled it alone."

Dani pursed her lips and nodded. "You're probably right." She gave me a small, mischievous smile. "But that doesn't mean I can't give you guidance. So long as you're asking the questions, they should be none the wiser."

I returned her smile. "Thank you. I can use all the advice I can get."

"What do you know so far?" Kim asked.

I shrugged. "Not a lot. The victim's first name is Avery. And it apparently happened at an apiary."

"Huh." Heather tapped her fingers against the table. "I used to buy honey from a woman named Avery."

"Used to?" I asked.

Heather nodded. "She was never the friendliest, but about a month ago, she got more prickly than usual. I decided to give a few of the other local apiaries a try."

"How many are there?" Dani asked.

Heather shrugged. "At least six that I've found, although some are more like backyard setups than something that could supply a bakery. I might have to look for something on the peninsula if this next one doesn't work out."

"So, where are you going to start?" Kim asked.

I glanced at my watch. "I have a meeting with Victor in about forty-five minutes. Chris recommended I talk to him first."

"That sounds great." Dani pulled a notepad from her purse and began jotting things down. "In the few cases I poked around in, I usually started with talking to family and friends. It helped me identify who might hold a grudge. Looking over the scene was always helpful too. Especially if I could use the spell that helped me look into the past. Do you have an obsidian mirror?"

I held still and tried to keep the panic from showing in my eyes. While I could technically cast spells from any of the schools of magic, divination was one of my weakest areas. I could charm someone easily, but anything that required me to look beyond what I could see with my own eyes made me feel like I was wading through mud.

What was I expecting to do—just smile at people and ask nicely if they killed her? Now I get to look like a fool in front of my coven. They're going to realize I'm a fraud and replace me. No. No... they are my friends. They wouldn't do that. Calm down.

Dani looked up at me. "I can loan you my obsidian mirror if you don't have one."

Kim glanced between the two of us and leaned forward to capture Dani's attention. "Why don't we work on ideas that play to her strengths? I've been fiddling with a truth spell with my daughter. It's not done yet, though."

Heather nodded and grabbed Dani's notepad. She jotted down a few more things. "I don't know about the magic angle, but I've helped out on a few of these investigations too. Checking social media has been surprisingly helpful, both for list making and clue finding."

They handed the notepad back and forth a few more times, each adding another item to it. After about a minute, Dani slid it across to me so I could read the full list.

Interview Family and Friends
Inspect Crime Scene
Check Social Media
Make Suspect List
Interview Suspects
Snoop Around Suspects' Homes and Work

I reread the list, my eyes darting back and forth as I took in the notes next to them about determining method, motive and opportunity. It was a lot. It was too much.

My mouth went dry. *How am I supposed to get all this done and still take care of Gertie?*

My familiar, a large dairy cow, was fortunately low-maintenance. But that didn't mean she required no maintenance. If I focused on every item on this list, I wouldn't have enough time to take care of her and my chickens or water and weed the crops I'd planted earlier in the month. I didn't know what I'd been thinking when I agreed to take on the liaison position.

Oh right. Never say no to a warden. Which unspoken rule is that again? I sighed and pinched the bridge of my nose.

Kim patted my shoulder. "I'll have my kids go out to help out on the farm while you tackle all this. Lindsey's been wanting to get into agricultural science anyway, so it'll be a good experience for her. And Conner just has too much energy. He could use a few hours of mucking out stalls and pulling weeds."

Of the three of my coven members, she was the one who knew me the best. I squeezed her hand. "Thanks."

"I'll help too. It's been a while since I've fed chickens, but I'm sure I can figure it out," Dani said. "I'll check with my daughter Grace too. I'm not sure how much time she'll have. She's neck deep in preparing to go to that witch's college in Louisiana, but she might be able to squeeze in a few hours here and there between spell practice."

Heather ducked her head. "I would offer, but this place eats all my free time. But I can promise to always have a pot of coffee on for you."

The tension that had been slowly building up in my lower back released, and I sank into my seat. I smiled at each of my coven mates. We had been through a lot together, and they weren't going to abandon me now. Even if that had been my experience for most of my life, things were different now—my coven mates had my back. *Stop panicking over nothing.*

"Thank you."

My phone buzzed in my pocket, reminding me of my upcoming meeting. I tore off the list, lurched to my feet, and stumbled toward the door. "On that note, I gotta head out to meet with Victor. I wouldn't want to keep him waiting."

Talking to people this often was still new to me. And talking to someone as sweet as Victor always made me queasy. The butterflies in my stomach did a somersault as I trudged out to my truck. I did my best to ignore them as I drove.

The funeral home was a cute craftsman-style house painted warm beige with soft off-white highlights. The only things that revealed the building's true nature were an odd chimney in the back—for the crematorium—an understated sign in the front yard, and a hearse parked under a carport off to the side. I found a spot across the street and made my way to the front door.

I let myself into the foyer, where the colors from the exterior continued. Everything was either a warm wood or a calming tan. Straight ahead was a waist-high counter with a silver bell. To my right was a sitting area with an old-fashioned fainting couch, along with more comfortable love seats and chairs, and to my left was a larger room with rows of seats for funeralgoers. Normally, a funeral home would not be calming, but something about all the thoughtful touches Victor had put into the place instantly put me at ease. The butterflies in my stomach settled as I stopped in front of the counter and tapped the silver bell.

"Be right there!" Victor yelled in his smooth baritone.

"Take your time!" I shouted back.

I meandered away from the counter and peered at the art pieces hung along the walls. They depicted local scenery. I was studying a painting of Deception Pass when the floorboards creaked behind me. I glanced over my shoulder, and the butterflies in my stomach swirled again as Victor came into sight. He had taken off his usual Regency-era coat and replaced it with a lab coat. His white hair had been styled into his iconic pompadour, and his equally white beard had been neatly trimmed. He smiled at me, the warmth of it filling his blue eyes.

I wet my lips and turned toward him. "Did, um, did Chris let you know I was coming?"

Victor cocked his head and stepped back toward the hallway. "That he did. I hadn't heard about you joining the sheriff's department. Are congratulations in order?"

I tucked my hair behind my ears and followed him. "Not the sheriff's department. I'm a city employee. I just started today."

We stopped outside a steel door that looked out of place in the otherwise normal-looking residential hallway.

"I was about to start the autopsy. Did you want to wait out here?" he asked.

My eyes flicked between him and the door. In my work on a farm, I had handled my fair share of dead animals over the years, but a dead person was a very different beast. I shrugged. "Maybe?"

Victor gave me another one of his smiles and gestured to a door a few feet away. "If you want, you can sit in that room. It's for identifying bodies—I thought it might be too hard for family members to be in the same room. I can keep the blinds down and talk to you while I work. There's an intercom."

"Sounds good." I slipped into the room he'd indicated and took a seat.

The space was barely larger than a closet. It had a couple of chairs, and a long window covered one wall. As promised, Victor pulled the blinds down to obstruct my view.

A few seconds later, his warm voice spoke over the intercom. "I'm mostly going to be talking to myself, for the recording. But if you have any questions, pipe up at any time, all right?"

I nodded before realizing that he couldn't see me. "Got it."

From there, he began making observations. Avery had a large contusion on her forehead and dirt under her nails. Based on her body temperature and stiffness of the body, he was placing the time of death sometime between ten o'clock at night and midnight. His voice was melodic as he went through the steps. I fidgeted in my seat as he announced that he was about to make the first incision. And then static filled the line.

"What the—" Victor's voice was cut off as something loud clattered against the floor.

"Victor?" I stood and slid closer to the glass.

"Oh my god," Victor croaked, his voice pained. Something else clanged loudly.

This is why Miranda was so sure this was her case.

My stomach clenched, and I pushed myself away from the glass. I sprinted from the witness room to the steel door that led to the examination room. My sweaty palms slid against the handle until my fingers found purchase, and I yanked the door open. I stood and stared, slack-jawed, at the sight in front of me—Victor crouched, huddled against the wall, holding a metal pan up between him and the exam room table. Avery lay, mostly covered by a white sheet, with a swarm of bees erupting out of her chest where her heart would be. The buzzing intensified as the bees turned as one and surged toward me.

CHAPTER 3

"Calm." I threw my hands up and poured my magic into the word. It wasn't a practiced spell, but my intent was clear enough.

Every witch's magic looked different. Mine took the shape of translucent red petals. They swirled out of me and swept around the bees until it was hard to tell where the bees started and the petals began. The swarm slowed and hung in the air.

I glanced at Victor. His head was bowed, and his eyes were wide and staring.

"What's going on? That's not normal." Victor's voice cracked.

While he might not have been able to see the red flower petals, because only witches could see another witch's magic, he could still see that the swarm had erupted out of a woman's chest and was flying lazily in a circle in the middle of the room. I grimaced. *Just what I needed—another check in the Freak column. How am I going to look him in the eye after this?*

The buzzing became louder as the bees inched toward me. I focused on them. Worries about Victor had seeped into my magic. I forced the anxiety to the back of my mind and poured more of my will into control over the swarm. I couldn't stand there all day—I needed to contain them. My gaze bounced around the room, looking for someplace to store the group until a beekeeper could come and relocate them. My eyes landed on an open morgue drawer at the back of the room.

I pointed toward it. "In there."

The bees wavered for a second.

I pushed more of my will into the order. "In there now."

As one, the bees turned and flew straight into the morgue drawer. I sprinted across the room and slammed the metal door shut, sealing them inside.

"That isn't normal," Victor babbled behind me. "Bees aren't supposed to be inside someone. What was that? How did they get there?"

I inched toward him and kneeled in front of him. I put my hand on the metal pan. He didn't fight me as I lowered it until he could see my face. "Victor?" I murmured.

He swallowed. His eyes were somehow even wider than they'd been when I entered. Words tumbled out of his mouth in rapid succession. "She had honey in her veins. How does a woman live with honey in place of blood? How is that even possible?"

"Victor?" I murmured again.

He blinked and focused on my face.

"It's going to be okay. The bees are contained." I wet my lips. "I'm going to find a beekeeper who can come out and relocate them. Do you need anything until they get here?"

Victor's blue eyes bored into me. "How did you do that?"

I smiled sheepishly. "I'm a farmer, remember? Makes me good with animals."

"Are you not normal too?"

The bottom of my stomach dropped out, and my heart sank. My mouth opened and closed as I searched for words.

What on earth am I supposed to tell him? I wish I knew how to talk to people better. Tears formed in my eyes.

I backed away and pulled out my phone. "I should find that beekeeper for you."

"I—I didn't mean it in a bad way." Victor pushed himself away from the wall. "Normal is overrated anyway."

I dialed Miranda and held up my hand, motioning for him to wait while I created more space between us. I didn't know what sort of woman had a hive for a heart, either, but I suspected Miranda would. Before I got a beekeeper out here to relocate the hive, I wanted to make sure it would be safe for them to do so.

"Miranda Blackwood."

I turned my back on Victor and lowered my voice. "She had bees inside her."

Miranda hummed. "I was worried something like that would happen. Dryad physiology can be strange at times."

"Why didn't you warn me?" I hissed.

"There are at least seventeen different types of dryad hearts, some of which look almost completely normal. Which one was I supposed to warn you about? Since I don't hear buzzing in the background, it sounds like you've figured it out well enough on your own."

"Well enough on my own? I've corralled them into a morgue drawer!" I glanced over my shoulder and inched farther away from Victor. I dropped my voice until it was barely above a whisper. "And… what about Victor? How is he supposed to finish the autopsy if he doesn't know what he's looking for?" *Can he even finish it? How different is her anatomy?*

"I'll take care of that," Miranda said.

My body stiffened, and I held myself perfectly still. "Take care of it how? The council gave me authority over containment in the field."

"Don't worry about it. He'll be fine. I'm sure you'll figure out a way to contain it appropriately." Miranda sighed. "Is that all?"

I grumbled at her for another minute before disconnecting the call. After spending so much of my life dealing with people directing their ire at me for simply existing, I'd grown hyperaware of when I was being watched. I could feel Victor studying me from across the room. He wasn't looking at me with hatred, though. All I felt in his gaze was curiosity. But I still didn't know what to say to him. I straightened my spine in an attempt to hide my nerves, and typed out a message to Heather.

> You mentioned beekeepers this morning. You know any that would be willing to come collect a rogue swarm?

Heather didn't miss a beat.

> **Heather:**
> I do...

> What happened?

> Avery was something called a dryad. Apparently, they sometimes have hives for hearts. I have the bees in a morgue drawer, but I'm worried the cold will kill them.

> **Heather:**
> I know someone. I'll ask them to head over ASAP.

Before today, I hadn't heard of a dryad outside of Greek mythology. And even then, my knowledge had ended at tree spirit. I thought they were supposed to have green hair or something, but Avery looked so normal. On the outside, anyway. I doubted Heather had known much either, but she always rolled with the situation as if the strange things we introduced her to were normal.

Without anything else to delay the inevitable, I shoved my phone into my pocket and turned back to Victor, who was staring at me like I was a puzzle he was trying to solve.

I cleared my throat. "Someone should be by soon to assist with the bees."

Victor nodded. "What does containment mean?"

I stared at him, my jaw clamped shut. *How do I respond to that?* Boldly stating that I could modify memories and being faced with having to do it were two different things. His quizzical blue eyes held my gaze, his expression trusting.

"Was I not supposed to see that?" he asked.

I jerked my head to the side in a stiff shake.

He shoved his hands into his coat pockets and rocked back on his heels. "What are you?"

"A witch."

"Are you going to cast some sort of spell on me?"

I grimaced. "I—you're not supposed to remember things like this."

"Okay. Before you do anything, can we take a minute to talk?"

I couldn't get my body to move. I was frozen in place, staring at him, as he waited for me to respond.

He took my silence as an answer. "I'm going to make some assumptions. Let me know if I'm off base. Avery McGlynn isn't human, and someone—maybe Chris, maybe someone in the city government—knew that, and that's why you're here."

I nodded.

"You're new to the job… it's to investigate crimes involving things like her."

"Sort of."

He nodded. "And containment means making me forget I saw this."

"Yes."

He inhaled deeply and let it out in a slow stream. "You don't look like you want to."

His expression was open and trusting. I clenched my fists at my sides. Tears pricked at the back of my eyes. I mentally measured the distance between us. The only reason he was looking at me like that was because he was within the field of my influence. Anyone within ten feet of me tended to like me more than they should, unless they had a good reason not to. *How is this not a good reason?*

"Do you want to?" he whispered.

"No. But... it's my job now."

"Have you done it to me before?"

I took a half step back. I had used the spell a handful of times when people had trespassed onto my property and saw things they shouldn't have. But never like this. Never to a friend. "No."

"Mind if I make some arguments against it?"

A lump formed in my throat, and I nodded robotically.

He held up his hand with a single finger raised. "Reason number one—if you have a role like this, logic dictates that there must be sufficient preternatural crime to support that role. It would be more useful for you if I were in the know. If something strange like this crosses my desk again, I know who to call."

That's a good point. I continued to stare at him.

He ticked off another finger. "Reason number two—well, more of an expansion of one, but I feel it is strong enough on its own. If I am in the know, I can learn things about the preternatural and would be able to give useful insights after autopsies. I assume that if you'd had your own expert, Avery wouldn't have ended up here."

Is that what Miranda meant when she said she would take care of it? Do the Wardens have a local expert? Wouldn't she have said something? I internally scoffed. She wouldn't. Miranda kept everything close to the chest. It almost felt like she was waiting for me to fail. I gritted my teeth. *Maybe I do need my own expert.*

"Reason number three—you're a good person, and I clearly don't want to forget this. I want to remember that you're special too. I think you would feel guilty about doing this. And I don't want that for you." He dropped his hand after ticking off the third finger and held my gaze, daring me to respond. "I propose that you let me keep my memories, at least for now. We can revisit this discussion later. And in the meantime, I get back to the autopsy."

"I—" *What other differences does a dryad have? Beetles for bones? Will he find anything useful? What if he does?* I exhaled slowly. "Okay. I would just proceed with caution."

Victor circled the table.

Should I watch? Would he even want me in the room after what just happened? How can he look so comfortable around me, knowing I can change his memories?

I needed to get out of there. I pulled out the checklist my coven had put together. I didn't know who her family and friends were just yet, so I skipped down to the next item. *Inspect the crime scene.*

"Where was she found?" I asked.

Victor rattled off an address as he replaced his exam gloves. "You'll probably need an ATV to get up to the house. The tree growth up there is very dense, and there isn't a road for the last mile."

"Thanks." I gave the morgue drawer one last glance before turning on my heel and marching toward the door with my head held high.

"Oh, and Megan?"

I stiffened then glanced over my shoulder at him.

"Thank you for making an exception. I'm good at keeping things to myself, so… your secret is safe with me."

I nodded and pushed my way through the door. My internal mantra, *Don't show your nerves,* played on repeat until

I made it to my truck, where I collapsed into the front seat and closed my eyes. *Did I make the right choice?* Victor's parting words echoed in my ears. My secret was safe with him. *Does he mean it?* Only time would tell.

I put my truck into gear and pulled away from the curb. As much as I wanted to sit and contemplate my decisions, I had a job to do. Nothing new was going to come of me twirling in circles inside my own head.

Inspect the crime scene. Interview family and friends. I mentally went through the list as I drove back toward my farm.

While my truck had good off-road capabilities, it would be useless in an area with thick trees. I didn't have an ATV, but I did have something better for getting into hard-to-reach areas: Gertie, my dairy cow familiar. As an added bonus, she was always calming to be around. And at the moment, I desperately needed her to help me focus on the case instead of wondering why Victor had used the word *special* to describe me.

CHAPTER 4

Gertie's saddle had been custom-made. When I'd contacted a local craftsman to commission the piece, they thought I was joking. No one in their right mind got a saddle for a cow. Their opinion had shifted when they came out to take her measurements and saw her size for the first time. Gertie, from a distance, looked like a standard dairy cow. Up close, she was anything but. Witch familiars were always large for their breed. Dani's cat, Charlie, was easily thirty pounds and came up past her knees. Being an abnormally large dairy cow meant Gertie was almost the size of a Clydesdale horse. She was well over five and half feet at the shoulder, and her broad back took some getting used to. She shifted under me as she trundled along, plodding her way through the trees. Through our bond, I could sense her curiosity. She wanted to stop and sniff everything because we hadn't ridden out to this part of the island before. I suspected she walked slowly so she could smell all the good scents instead of rushing past them before she got a chance to enjoy them.

I patted Gertie on the shoulder as we emerged from the thickest part of the woods into a large clearing filled with native flowers. A white picket fence encircled it a few feet in from the tree line. At the center was a redbrick cottage half covered in ivy. A few feet from the front door was a cluster of wooden beehive boxes. My breath caught in my throat as I stared at the home. It looked as if it had been lifted from the pages of a fairy tale. *Idyllic* didn't even begin to describe how adorable the house was.

Gertie ground to a halt and snorted. I tapped her sides with my heels, urging her onward, and she shook her head and stepped back.

I leaned forward over her shoulder and scratched her ears. "Did you want to wait by the fence?"

Gertie inched forward and stopped next to one of the fence posts. She stared over the white-painted points, uneasiness rolling off her in waves. This was the first time she had ever been brought to a place where someone had died. She could probably smell the violence. I slipped off her back and patted her side. As I moved past her to the gate, she nuzzled my shoulder.

Walking toward the home, I studied the ground. My dad —before my mom died and he fled—had taken me hunting. I focused on the task at hand, trying to keep the memories at bay. My mom's death had resulted in the loss of two parents —my mom, to the ground, and my dad when her spell to keep him there had broken. We never talked about it, but part of me had thought that despite it all and despite the curse, he'd been there because he wanted to be. It was a rude awakening to realize he'd never loved me. Couldn't love me. And I never wanted something that fake again. It was too hard.

I exhaled slowly and blinked at my feet. It had been a while since I'd had to study tracks, but these were clear enough. Three separate sets of footprints tromped through the wildflowers. The largest set, easily at least a size fifteen, reminded me of Deputy Abbott. He was too long of limb and gangly. Over the past year, he had started to grow into his frame so he looked a little bit less like a guy who had been stretched out like Laffy Taffy and more like a basketball player. The second set had the same tread pattern but was smaller, maybe a size ten. The stride was measured. Mentally, I labeled those steps Sheriff Harris. The last set of footprints had a smoothness that screamed loafers.

Victor. My heart tightened at the thought of what Miranda might be doing to him. *Will she change his memories anyway?* If she did, I doubted she would be as gentle as I would have been.

I shook my head and tried to focus as I continued padding forward. When I encountered the first evidence cone, I stopped. Glancing up, I took in the rest of the clearing. The cones were half hidden by the flowers, which lay in a sporadic pattern around the beehives. I inched my way around the crime scene. *What am I supposed to be looking for?* My shoulders ached from me fighting the urge to hunch. Every muscle in my back was tight as I continued my slow circle around the crime scene. I let my gaze bounce from cone to cone, trying to determine a pattern or find something useful in the chaos. I took a few steps back, wondering if seeing it all from a distance would help. As a fourth set of footprints came into view to my left, I paused. Cocking my head, I padded toward them.

While Victor and company had approached the hives from the gate, these footsteps emerged from the woods on the opposite side of the home. The tread was bigger than Chris's but smaller than Deputy Abbott's. They were much too large to have belonged to Avery. I followed them to the tree line. They were difficult to make out over the field of flowers. There was a small section, between the field and the forest, where the ground was muddy and the footprints were clear. Then whoever made them had stepped onto a hard-packed game trail, and the prints disappeared. I stared at three that were clear. None of them was perfect, but with a little magic, I could create a foot mold of the left shoe from the two partial prints.

I snapped a few pictures and then clenched and unclenched my hands as I prepared to cast. It was a spell my mom had taught me. With so few handymen willing to come out to assist on the farm, we'd had to get creative. When something broke, we would fix it ourselves, which sometimes required us to create parts. I learned how to make molds from broken pieces, using a transformation spell. While it wasn't my strong suit, I was no slouch when it came to the magic of change.

I muttered the familiar words. A section of mud a few feet away lifted into the air and then settled over the footprints. The translucent red petals of my magic sank into the mud, staining it red. I continued to murmur as the reddened mud rose back into the air, and the two partial prints flew together. They flashed and then hardened into a single perfect footprint. I reached out and plucked it from the air.

I slipped my backpack off my shoulders and tucked the mold into one of the side pockets. With the evidence secured, I made my way back to the cluster of evidence cones. As I approached, the buzzing from the hives grew steadily louder. I slowed my pace and studied the boxes. There weren't any bees outside, but the buzzing grew louder. It took on an angry edge as my toes moved past the farthest cone from the center. I took a step back, and the sound quieted slightly. I cocked my head and inched forward again. The angry buzzing intensified with each step until bees surged out of the hives en masse and swarmed around the boxes—almost like they were creating a barrier between me and whatever lay at the center.

Holding my hand up, I pulled on my will and sent calming waves of magic toward them. My red petals hit the swarm and crumbled. The buzzing ratcheted up from angry to furious. The hair on the back of my neck stood up as millions of eyes focused on me. My mouth went dry, and I scrambled backward. The swarms shifted as if all the bees wanted to keep me in view. They hung in the air between me and Gertie. No wonder she didn't want to come closer.

I steadied my breathing, my hands clenching and unclenching at my sides. I held the rest of my body still as I studied them. I shifted to my left, and they followed. There was no way I was getting any closer without them surrounding me. Inch by inch, I made my way around them. With each step, I studied their movements. So long as I didn't get any closer, they appeared to be content to let me move.

What am I supposed to do now? I am so out of my depth here. I took another half step and hit the side of the cottage. The buzzing intensified, and the bees rose higher and flew toward me. I flung myself to the side as they collided with the building. I scrambled away on all fours then ran for the only place I could take cover: the cottage.

Holding my hand out in front of me, I yelled a quick spell to unlock and open the front door. The hand-carved wooden door flew open, and I fell inside. I surged to my feet, spun in place, and slammed the door behind me as the swarm rallied and tried to follow. The door shut just in time. Bees hit it in such large numbers the sound of their tiny bodies slamming against the wood reverberated through the room. I flipped the lock and scrambled around the building to make sure all the doors and windows were closed. At the last second, I threw a fire spell into the hearth, lighting the small pile of wood, to keep the bees out of the chimney. I sank to my knees and collapsed against the wall, my heart beating rapidly.

"What on earth? That wasn't normal." My head fell back. I closed my eyes and collected my thoughts. The bees were acting strange, but they belonged to a dryad.

Would a dryad with a hive for a heart change bee behavior? I would assume so. Maybe they're grieving. Do bees grieve? Think,

Megan. I should just call Miranda and give the case to her. That would be the simple solution.

I shook my head and pushed myself to stand. I was a Miller, and Millers were used to things being complicated. We didn't take the easy way out.

I turned slowly in place, taking in my surroundings. The cottage was small but functional. On one side was a kitchen with dark wood cabinetry and on the other a small living room. A large island bisected the space. A fireplace took up most of the far wall. A spiral staircase with a hand-carved banister led up to the loft that overlooked the space, with a queen-sized bed and a cozy-looking chair and low bookshelves on all sides. The only electrical things in the whole place were a landline attached to the wall, a couple of standard kitchen appliances—an oven and a fridge—and an old-fashioned radio that sat on the table in the breakfast nook. There wasn't even a microwave. The space was homey, and I could feel Avery's personality through every personal touch, from the art on the walls to the embroidered hand towel hanging in the kitchen. She was clearly someone who liked doing things herself.

I mentally went through my coven's list for how to investigate a murder. At the bottom of the list was snooping around the victim's home and/or work. Based on the rows of empty honey jars and the Avery's Apiary labels stacked on the kitchen counter, it was clear that the cottage was both home and workplace. I took a step into the living room and let my eyes wander a bit more. On first inspection, the space was a little cluttered, but as my eyes swept past the various stacks of papers and other items, it became clear that everything had its place.

I walked into the kitchen and quickly looked through the various items. One section of the counter was covered with supplies for bottling honey and another with gardening items. I sifted through the wide assortment of flower seeds, large tubs filled with different types of soil, and fertilizer. I peered into one that almost looked gray before moving on to the next section of the counter, which was overflowing with paper. I ran my fingers over the stacks of paper. The first consisted of order slips. Next to it was a ledger. I started to note down names, but the task soon became unwieldy. She sold honey to people and businesses all over the island. I took a few photos of the pages and moved on to the next stack, which appeared to be a volunteer packet for one of the city council members' campaigns.

I flipped the packet open. On the first page was a head shot of the candidate, with her name in bold letters underneath. Amanda Yu looked to be about my age—in her late thirties, maybe early forties. Her jet-black hair was cut into a severe bob that made her sharp jawline more pronounced. She was angular, with dark-gray eyes that seemed to stare right into mine. Despite her austere styling, the warmth in her smile brightened her face into an expression both businesslike and inviting.

When a twig cracked in the yard, my head snapped toward the kitchen window. I dropped the packet and scrambled over to look outside. The man wasn't as close to the house as I'd thought but was well past the tree line, approaching on foot. He was average height with a sturdy build. He wore a pair of dark-blue jeans and a tan button-up shirt. I looked between him and the hives. In the few minutes I had been inside the house, the bees had retreated to their boxes, but I had the feeling if he got much closer, they would reemerge. I dashed to the door and ran out to meet him.

He faltered when he saw me, his expression shifting from startled to friendly in half a second. He strode past the white picket fence, his hand outstretched to shake mine. "I don't think I've seen you around these parts before."

"You should step back. It's an active crime scene over here." I guided him back beyond the fence.

He blinked, his mouth frozen in a smile before shifting to a concerned frown. "A crime scene? I thought I saw the sheriff's car over here this morning when I was headed into town and came over to make sure everything was all right when I got back in. I didn't want to be one of those neighbors, you know—too nosy during times of stress. Is Miss McGlynn okay?"

I grimaced. "No. She... she was found dead this morning. How well did you know Avery?"

"Not well. She seemed nice enough but largely kept to herself." He shoved his hands into his pockets and rocked back on his heels. "I feel like a bad neighbor. I moved into my father's old farmhouse about a year ago and just haven't had the time to introduce myself properly. First with cleaning up the place and then with the campaign. I'd hoped to rectify that when things calmed down a little, you know?"

"Campaign?"

"City council." He flashed me a sad smile. "It was one of my dad's dreams. I guess you could say I'm trying to honor his memory. He really loved this town."

"You must love it, too, if you're willing to dive into town politics."

"What's not to love?" He held his hands out. "Anyway, I don't think I caught your name, Miss...?" He raised one of his eyebrows.

"Megan." I held my hand out to him. "Megan Miller. I'm doing some work for the city."

His hand was warm. I could tell a lot about a person by their hands. He had a firm handshake, but his skin was smooth. He was someone who'd spent most of his life working from behind a desk but probably had a position in management. He was too sure of himself to be involved in any grunt work for long.

"John Barfield."

I had seen a few of his campaign posters around town. I

released his hand. "As someone running for city council, you probably have your ear to the ground, right?"

"You could say that." His smile widened.

"I thought so. While you may not have known Avery well yourself, I'm sure you've heard things about her."

He nodded.

"Did anyone ever mention her having problems with anyone?"

He furrowed his brow in thought. "It's probably nothing, but now that you mention it, while standing in line at the feed store, I heard that she recently had a falling-out with a friend. Jennifer? Jasmine? I know her name started with a *J*. She runs Moon and Mortar, a little apothecary shop downtown. From what I understand, they used to be like two peas in a pod, but they had some sort of falling-out a few weeks back. It's allegedly been bad blood ever since. But... you didn't hear that from me. I don't want my potential future constituents thinking I'm a gossip."

I mimed zipping my lips. "If it was being talked about at the feed store, I could have heard it anywhere. Thanks for the information."

He nodded and took a step back. "I'll let you get to it, then."

I watched as he walked over to an ATV parked about ten feet into the tree line, between a massive gray oak and a pile of white rocks. He waved and climbed aboard. The ATV engine growled as he backed out and disappeared into the forest.

I made my way over to Gertie and patted her on the shoulder before slipping my foot into the stirrup and throwing my other leg up and over her back. I turned her toward town. I was familiar with Moon and Mortar but had never been inside. I was still getting used to being welcome in town, so I hadn't made it to the apothecary store's grand opening a few months prior.

I debated taking Gertie back home, but by the time I did that, switched out to my truck, and drove back into town, the store might not still be open. I guided Gertie with my knees. While it wasn't common for people to ride horses into town, it did happen on occasion. And if people really were going to be welcoming me into the community, they would have to get used to seeing her around. Riding a cow wasn't that different from riding a horse.

"Let's go interview our first suspect," I murmured.

CHAPTER 5

Moon and Mortar was located four blocks inland from the pier, at the very edge of the historical downtown, and had only recently been swept up in Steven Bishop's revitalization efforts. He had been the town's mayor for just over a year, and he had run on the promise that he wouldn't let our downtown languish as it had under the last mayor. So far, he had fulfilled his promises and then some. When he'd taken over, almost a third of the storefronts a block away from the boardwalk had been shuttered. Now an empty storefront was a rare sight.

I guided Gertie to a parking spot out front and hopped down. I stroked her nose. "Stay here. I'll be back in a few minutes."

Gertie laid her head on my shoulder and huffed into my ear. She was content enough to wait, but she let me know she wanted a few cow cookie treats when we got back home.

I scratched under her chin. "You got it."

I turned and strode into the store. Just inside the door, I paused, waiting for my eyes to adjust. Most of the lights were turned down low. The walls were lined with shelves that held rows of jars of dried herbs, with stacks of empty wax-paper baggies stashed in little alcoves underneath. Small hand-carved wooden flowers hung from twine above the windows. Tables were scattered around the room, with purple-and-gold tablecloths draped over them. I faltered when my gaze landed on a painting on the back wall. In it, a woman with a mane of black hair stood in front of the moon, branches crowding around her. Her green eyes stared straight at me. I recognized the painting, and I recognized the space I was in. It had been remodeled, but it used to belong to a medium before she was murdered over her ability to see and talk to ghosts.

Floorboards creaked in the back of the store. I tore my eyes away from the painting and glanced toward the sound. A woman had emerged from the back of the store, carrying a tray full of teapots. Her wavy chestnut hair hung loose around her shoulders. She was dressed in a black maxi dress with a sunflower pattern.

She smiled at me as she set the tray down. "Welcome to the Moon and Mortar. I don't think I've seen you in here before."

I wound my way through the tables and came to a stop a few feet away from her. "It's my first time in. At least since it changed ownership. I'm Megan."

"Jessica." She shook my hand. "Was there something in particular you were looking for?"

I smiled at her weakly. "I was hoping I could ask you some questions. Do you have a few minutes to talk?"

She grabbed one of the teapots and deposited it on a nearby table. "So long as you don't mind me working while we talk. I have my Tea and Tarot event starting in about thirty minutes, and I still need to finish setting up. What did you want to talk about?"

I stepped to the side and let her work. "Avery McGlynn."

She froze for a second before dropping off the next teapot and returning to the tray. "What about Avery?"

I cleared my throat. *Maybe I should have asked for more guidance on how to interview people. Am I supposed to do small talk first? Have I already bungled this? Just be direct. There's no use backpedaling now.* "I understand you recently had a falling-out with her and was curious to hear what happened."

She sagged and stood with her back to me. "I wish I knew. I thought we were best friends."

I swallowed. My thoughts scattered. I couldn't figure out what to say next.

Jessica turned and folded her arms over her stomach. "Ten years, we were friends. Ten years, and it all just went away like that." She snapped her fingers. She snorted and shook her head. "If you want to know the reason, you should ask Avery. And if she bothers to tell you, would you let me know? My son, Liam, is heartbroken. I'm not sure what to tell him. He keeps asking if he can go play hide-and-seek with her, and I keep coming up with excuses not to let him."

I did my best to school my features, but something must have slipped through. Her expression shifted from melancholy to concerned. She stepped forward, her hand reaching for me. Her fingers hovered a few inches from my arm.

"Did something happen?" she asked.

"I'm sorry. It's just, I can't ask Avery. I'm not sure how to say this... she's dead."

She gasped and covered her mouth, her eyes going wide. "What?"

"She was found this morning. The sheriff asked me to look into it."

She sat down hard, her fingers clutching the empty teapot she held against her chest. "I suppose that makes sense. Megan Miller, right? Of Miller Farms?" She glanced up at me as I nodded. "I like Chris, but he probably doesn't know the first thing about dryads."

My jaw dropped, and I took the seat opposite her. "You knew?"

"Best friends, remember?" Jessica closed her eyes. "She told me a few years ago when she realized what I was. I'm not a powerful witch by any stretch of the imagination. I've got some skill over hearth-and-home stuff. Mostly abjuration, with a smattering of conjuration thrown in. We bonded over our connection to nature."

My mind reeled. Jessica was a witch. She knew I was a witch. *How does she know?* I held myself perfectly still in the chair, my back ramrod straight.

She wiped at her eyes and stood. "I'm just glad it's you and not Miranda. The Wardens have always given me the creeps. I know I'm not alone in that. The city council must be thrilled to have you on board."

I relaxed a hair. That made sense. *Of course Miranda would have given the local supernatural community a heads-up. How am I supposed to be a liaison if they don't know who I am and I don't know who they are? I bet Miranda has a list and neglected to give it to me. Or did she want me to look foolish?*

"I'm assuming, by your questions, foul play is suspected," Jessica said.

"Unfortunately." I stood and moved so I could see her face. "Can you think of anyone who would have wanted to hurt Avery?"

Jessica shrugged. "She'd been acting out of sorts lately."

"How so?"

Jessica grimaced. "I've never been one for gossip. Now I feel like I'm speaking ill of the dead. But... if it'll help... she'd been getting into a lot of arguments all over town over the past month. Cutting ties. I've never seen her so paranoid. And when I asked her about it, she cut me off. I kept hoping she would open back up, but she never did. We haven't spoken in a few weeks, so I'm not sure who would top the list anymore."

"Was Avery close to anyone else who might know?"

Jessica tapped her chin. "The only one left who she hadn't

cut out would probably be Diana. They seemed close in the past. And she was probably a bit harder to cut out than the rest of us since she lives on the property."

"Do you have her contact information?"

She shook her head. "She lived almost as off the grid as Avery. But she's almost always home. She retired a few years back. After her husband died it's just been her, her cats, and her paintings. She did that one." Jessica pointed to the painting of the woman on the back wall. "I can jot down the directions. She lives in a cabin that's attached to the orchard. The road access is just as bad as Avery's place." She glanced past me to Gertie standing in the parking stall. "You may need to ride out there. Cute cow."

I asked her a few more questions before wrapping up the interview. She didn't know anything else helpful. Avery was a dryad who'd rarely left her orchard. Her favorite food had been apple pie, and only the queen bees had names—Tempest, Raven, Medusa, and Regina. Apparently, Regina was moody, so Avery had named her after a character from one of her favorite movies. Jessica seemed legitimately saddened by Avery's passing, but I wasn't as skilled at reading those sorts of emotions. While I could tell when someone was angry or gearing up to become aggressive, I hadn't needed to be able to tell the difference between real or fake sadness or joy before. While I couldn't be sure I was reading her emotions correctly, Jessica didn't feel like a killer to me.

I mentally moved her name from the top of the suspect list to the bottom. All the other names were unknown, but they would get filled in eventually. Maybe Diana would point me in a more useful direction.

CHAPTER 6

The sun was hanging low in the sky by the time I reached the fence around Diana's home. The trek up here had been a little easier than the one to Avery's door, but not by much. Gertie had grumbled for the last quarter mile, her plodding steps becoming slower, until a tiny cabin appeared ahead of us. Trees loomed over the structure. It had the same style white picket fence around it as Avery's cottage and a similar vibe, except this was a log cabin and the yard was mostly moss. I slipped off of Gertie and trudged up the stone walkway to the front door. My knock sounded overly loud in the quiet of the forest.

The front door swung open, and my eyes tracked downward to a petite woman. She was maybe five feet tall. Her hair, more silver than brown, was piled on top of her head in a messy bun. She wore an oversized T-shirt that hung almost to her knees. It was paint speckled.

She peered up at me, her eyes red rimmed. "Can I help you?"

"Diana?"

She nodded and hugged her arms to her body, somehow becoming smaller. "That's me."

I held my hand out. "I'm Megan Miller. Sheriff Harris asked me to help him out on a case. Do you have a few minutes to answer some questions?"

Diana glanced behind me at the setting sun. Her body deflated further, and she stepped backward. She gestured weakly toward the kitchen table. "Please, come inside. Can I get you something to drink?"

I followed her in. The cabin was even smaller than Avery's place. The kitchen and living room were tiny. There was a short hallway with two doors. I suspected they were for the bedroom and the bathroom. The limited space was filled with art. Paintings sat stacked against the walls. In the center of the living room were a stool and an easel with the beginnings of a dark forest painting, the details indistinct.

Diana pointed to the small table. I hovered over the single chair as she grabbed the stool and pulled it over to sit down opposite me. With her seated, I claimed the chair.

"You said you were helping the sheriff with a case," Diana said.

"I'm not sure if you've heard, but Avery McGlynn was found dead this morning."

Diana hunched forward, her long fingers clasping together over her bony knees. "I'm aware. I called it in. I was wondering when someone would come by but had assumed it would be Chris or that tall fellow. Harrison? Are you some sort of detective, then? They must really trust you if they've tasked you with investigating a murder."

I tried not to flinch. I was still getting used to people trusting me. The word *trust* would always feel weighted. For the longest time, the only people who trusted me had been the ones I compelled to trust me through magic. The spell I used was designed to let people see me for who I really was, past my familial curse, but I never stopped wondering if it did more than that. People so quickly became my friend after drinking the spelled coffee that it was like emotional whiplash—enemies one second, friends the next. It had always felt too good to be true. And now people gave me their trust without a second thought. I wasn't sure if I deserved it.

I forced a polite smile and nodded. "I work for the city. I guess you could say these are other duties as assigned."

"Oh, like Victor? He asked me a couple questions before he left."

My stomach churned. I hadn't seen Victor since he'd discovered witches were real. I didn't know if I should be checking in on him. *What did Miranda do to him? Will he even remember our conversation?*

I pushed the thought aside. "What sort of questions?"

"Well, I suppose they weren't really investigative. He mostly wanted to make sure I was okay." She curled in on herself, and her voice softened to barely above a whisper. "He could tell I was hurting. But that man is used to seeing grief. He gave me some resources for grief counseling. I hated going after my husband died. But… it helped. I can't believe I'll have to go again."

"It sounds like you knew Avery well."

Diana wiped at her eyes. "She was like a daughter to me. She gave me—" Diana's head swung toward the kitchen window, and her mouth dropped open. "What on earth?"

I glanced behind me and met the expectant eyes of Gertie. She was peering at us through the window, her expression forlorn. "Gertie, what are you doing? You were supposed to wait by the fence."

Gertie snuffled at the window, her big brown eyes widening. She had the sad puppy-dog eyes down pat.

"Is that a cow? She's so cute."

I nodded and turned back around in my seat. "Her name's Gertie. Growing up, we didn't have space for a horse on the farm, so I learned how to ride her. She's just as good at getting around spots like this as an ATV."

Diana stood and crept toward the window. "I've never seen a cow that big before. Is she hungry?"

"Maybe a little." I smothered a laugh as Gertie's eyes managed to get even wider, and she shuffled forward until her nose was almost flush with the glass. "She's hamming it up a bit, hoping you'll give her something."

Diana smiled and grabbed an apple from the fruit bowl on the counter. "Mind if I give her an apple while we talk?"

"Go ahead."

Diana opened the window and quickly cut a slice of the apple. She handed over the slice, which Gertie took gently between her teeth. "So, how can I help you?"

"Did Avery have any enemies?"

Gertie stuck her head through the window, hitting one of the cabinets, in a bid to get more apple.

"Enemies?" Diana asked.

"Anyone she had arguments with that... could have gotten more heated than usual?"

Diana sighed and cut up more apple. She stood there, handing over apple slice after apple slice. "To be honest, Avery had pulled back a bit over the past few weeks. I thought she was too busy for me. Last we spoke, she was thinking about volunteering for Amanda Yu's campaign. And then she kind of fell out of contact. If I had to guess about anyone, based on what I heard around town and saw in the past, my money would be on either Travis Burrow or Russell Bennett."

"Why them?" I asked.

"I guess you could say Travis is a rival—was a rival—of Avery's. He's a beekeeper with a bit of a temper. I heard they got into a yelling match last week. And Russell is always getting worked up about the bees on the property. He was furious that she had added another hive."

"Do you know where I could find them?"

"I might have their information in my address book."

Diana handed off the last piece of apple and washed her hands. She dried them off on a fluffy kitchen towel before ducking into the hallway. "Let me check."

I was sitting in my chair, waiting for her to come back, when Gertie hit her head against the cabinet again. The door popped open, and a jar fell out and rolled across the counter into the trash.

"Gertie!" I whispered.

I scrambled to my feet and grabbed the jar from the trash can. It contained honey. I recognized the label from Avery's cottage. I paused with my hand around the jar as my eyes landed on a crumpled letter in the trash can. It was addressed to Avery.

Diana's humming got louder as the bedroom door opened. Instinctively, I mumbled the words to a minor confusion spell. It replicated the doorway effect—that feeling people got when they went into a room and forgot what they were there for. Most confusion spells were hard to predict, but this one almost always had the same effect—the target paused and maybe turned around. It bought me only a few seconds before their minds reengaged and they continued with what they were doing. But I didn't need long.

I held my breath, listening, as Diana stepped back inside the room and closed the door, her humming becoming fainter through the wood. I exhaled, shoved the jar of honey back into the cabinet, and fished the letter out.

Avery,

I've read your letter a dozen times now, and each time, I feel like the ground is slipping out from under me. I never imagined that you, of all people, would be the one to do this. I keep thinking there must be some misunderstanding, some way to fix this before it goes too far.

You've been like family to me for so many years. I watched you grow, celebrated your joys, shared in your struggles. I thought what we had between us was unshakable. That's why this hurts so deeply.

Please, Avery, don't go through with this. You may believe it's what has to be done, but you're not seeing what it's doing to me—to us. Once you take this step, things will never be the same again. I don't want to lose you.

I'm begging you to think again. Don't let this be the end of a decade of friendship. What can I do to get through to you? I've only ever wanted to be your friend.

D.

Diana's humming got louder as her the bedroom door reopened. I quickly snapped a photo of the letter and dropped it back into the trash can. I scrambled over to my seat and plopped down as she rounded the corner.

"I found the addresses you were looking for." Diana held up a scrap of paper. "Although, like I said, Travis can have a bit of a temper. I would approach him with caution if I were you."

She handed me the piece of paper. I glanced at the addresses. The handwriting matched the letter. There was no doubt in my mind that Diana had been writing to beg Avery to reconsider something. *Reconsider what?*

I tucked the paper into my pocket and rose from my seat. "Thank you."

We chatted for a few more minutes before I said good night and headed outside to take Gertie home. The sun had slipped lower on the horizon while I was inside. The sky was a riot of color as the sun set behind the trees. Under the branches, it felt like twilight had already begun.

I guided Gertie through the underbrush with my knees as I mentally went through the day. Jessica's sorrow felt too real. She was the lowest on my list of suspects. Diana had somehow found a place on the list. That letter was bizarre. I wasn't sure what to think about a rival beekeeper or a grumpy neighbor. I made a game plan for the next day. I would wake up early to tend to the farm and then head out to interview Russell and Travis.

CHAPTER 7

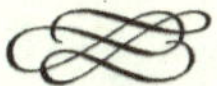

The morning passed in a blur. I crawled out of bed well before dawn and was elbow deep in farm chores when Lindsey and Conner, Kim's kids, showed up to lend a hand. They only had an hour before they had to go to school, but they threw themselves into the work with gusto. With all three of us working, I got through the list in record time. I was able to shower and head out for the day at a reasonable hour. I had two people to interview that day, and now I could do it without feeling rushed.

I'd taken some time to peek at the various social media accounts of the people on my list before bed the night before. Jessica's was full of posts about being a new business owner and the delights of being a mother to a rambunctious boy. Her takes on his antics were amusing. She had whole sections that reminded me of Steve Irwin—a study of a ten-year-old in his natural habitat. She seemed sweet, but at the same time, I couldn't help but notice that a month prior one or two posts a week had featured Avery, and then they didn't. John hadn't been wrong when he'd said they had a falling-out. They weren't even friends online anymore.

Avery's wall was bland and empty, other than posts where

someone else had tagged her. I couldn't tell if it was because she kept everything on a private setting or because she wasn't online much. Diana's was similar. She had a professional page that featured art, but it didn't look like she had shared any paintings in a few years—not since her husband had died.

Travis was online a lot. His posts ranged from talking about running a meadery to frequent flame wars with other island residents. He really did seem to have a temper and got worked up over the strangest things. Russell, on the other hand, was a blank slate other than a profile picture that hadn't been updated in at least ten years. But I did recognize him from the feed store. He had always come across as mild mannered and polite.

I opted to interview Russell first. Starting with the least intimidating person early in the morning seemed like a good idea. And I was willing to bet that someone who ran a meadery and got into flame wars at the drop of a hat was not a morning person.

Russell was Avery's closest neighbor. Even then, almost forty acres separated their homes. While I'd needed to ride Gertie up to Avery's house, Russell had a road that went straight to his property and was in good repair. I glanced at a map before heading out. Having been born and raised on Whidbey Island, I knew my way around and didn't need to rely on my GPS to get me where I was going.

I was approaching the turn onto his property when a truck parked at the side of the road caught my eye. I slowed and came to a stop next to a guy who was bent over, huffing and puffing, as he yanked a sign out of the ground. The man turned, and I recognized him immediately as Russell Bennett. His face was beet red around his graying blond beard. His unruly hair was only half contained under a baseball cap, and his flannel shirt and jeans were mud splattered. He squinted at me, and I waved and pulled over next to him.

"You're not out here to install another sign, are you?" Russell grumbled as I stepped out of my truck.

I glanced between his face and the crumpled campaign sign for John Barfield that he held loosely in his hands. I shook my head. "Nope. I was going to ask how you're doing this morning, but I can see it's not going well."

"I would be better if these dang signs would stop popping up in front of my house." He tossed it into the back of his truck. "I know, I know. This isn't technically my land. This small strip here is public property. But it's right in front of my house, and I don't want to be giving anyone any ideas about who I'm supporting in this election. Every time one of them appears out here, I have to deal with the other side's supporters harassing me into changing my position when I'm in town."

"Do you know who's doing it?" I asked.

Russell shrugged. "At first it was one of Amanda's people. But she was polite enough and stopped when I told her no. Whoever John has running his campaign has been less polite. I've been tearing these signs out like they're weeds."

I gave him a sympathetic smile and cleared my throat. "That sounds frustrating. Hopefully not so frustrating that you don't have a few minutes to talk."

"About what? It's not about this stupid election, is it?"

I shook my head. "I'm helping Chris out with an investigation."

Russell cocked an eyebrow and took off his hat. He squeezed the bill, forcing it into a more rounded shape. "An investigation? Huh. You didn't strike me as the investigating type. But who does? First it was that lady Chris got married to, and now it's you. Who's he going to deputize next—the broad who runs the Bizzy Bean?"

I didn't let my annoyance show on my face. "I just started a new job. I'm working for the city."

He nodded. "All right. Well, what do you want to know?"

"When did you last see Avery McGlynn?"

His chest puffed up. "Avery? What is she on about now? Just because I was walking near her property doesn't mean I went on it. I ain't no trespasser. She should know by now that I would never willingly set foot in her orchard. If she's filed some sort of formal complaint about that cockamamie story she's come up with, then I'll file one right back. She comes traipsing through here all the time without no invitation."

I blinked at him as I struggled to keep up. *Trespassing? Wait.* "Why would you never willingly set foot in her orchard?"

"Those blasted bees. I haven't been a fan of having so many of them this close for years. They keep flying onto my property. Stinging my cattle. They're menaces." He shuddered. "And then she had the audacity to get ten more hives. We had an agreement. Yeah, it may have been a verbal one, but I keep to those. Thirty-five hives maximum. Now she's at forty. Forty! There's going to be no avoiding them now."

"Her bees?" *Have they always been aggressive?*

"Yeah. Bees. I don't like 'em. There's a reason I do cattle and not flowers or produce of some sort. I can't stand the little buggers."

"Were her bees odd in same way?"

"Odd?" Russell shoved his cap back onto his head. "No. They're just bees. That's bad enough. Is that all?"

I wasn't any closer to figuring things out. My mind floundered for half a second before I remembered the mold I'd made of the footprint in my backpack. "Yeah. Mind if I take a look at your shoes?"

"My shoes? Why?"

"Avery was murdered, and I wanted—"

"Murdered?" Russell's jaw dropped. "And you... you're questioning me? Because I didn't like her bees?"

I kept my face impassive. The question did make it sound

ridiculous. But then again, having a feud over bees sounded ridiculous. As far as I knew, he'd made the whole thing up. "Can I look at your shoes?"

He shrugged and ambled over. He lifted his foot. I gestured for him to hold it out to the side so I could see the bottom and pulled the mold out of my bag. I held it up next to his boot. They were the same size, but Russell's boots were well-worn, the tread almost gone in some areas. The mold was of a newer boot.

"Anything else?" he asked.

"Did Avery have issues with anyone else?"

"Who didn't?" Russell shook his head. "She was as prickly as they came. It was like a personal insult that I didn't like her bees. With other people, it was a personal insult that they preferred a different color green. I don't mean to speak ill of the dead, but that woman would find a reason to be insulted with almost anyone. Her list of friends would be short."

I gave him a tight-lipped smile. "Thank you for your time."

I retreated to my truck and hoisted myself up into the front seat then studied him in the side view mirror. It was hard to tell who was the pricklier person in this scenario, Avery or Russell. Jessica had described her as changing over the past month.

Is Russell's opinion of Avery colored by her bees? I could understand her being hurt if someone didn't like what was very literally her heart. I squinted at him. *But how real is his dislike of bees? He could be trying to deflect.*

A small smile crossed my lips. His aversion to bees would be easy enough to verify. I muttered the words of a simple illusion spell and held the image of a bumblebee in my mind as I shaped the illusion. The image of the bee hung suspended in the air for a moment before it took flight. I added buzzing as it approached Russell. His head jerked around, and he stumbled back. All the color drained from his face as beads of sweat formed on his forehead, and he blinked rapidly.

As I watched his reaction, I lost my appetite. My chest tightened when he fell backward and scrambled on his elbows to get away. I guided the illusion away from him so he could flee to his truck. He ran to it, threw himself into the driver's seat, and slammed the door shut behind him. Russell didn't just dislike bees—he was terrified of them. I had a hard time picturing someone that afraid of bees willingly walking between Avery's hives to attack her. I lingered, making sure he drove away safely, before I pulled into the road. I tentatively took Russell off my list of suspects as I drove toward my next interview of the day—Travis Burrows, the rival beekeeper with anger-management issues.

CHAPTER 8

I peered out my truck window as I pulled to a stop in front of the sprawling rambler-style home. A massive wraparound porch curved around the entire house. A tire hung from a nearby tree by a corded rope. And all around the property were row upon row of bee boxes, with lavender stretching behind them for acres. Intermixed between the rows of lavender were other flowers and bird baths filled with glass beads.

My breath caught in my throat. It was beautiful, and the air was fragrant. I climbed out of my truck and turned toward the house as the front door slammed open and a beast of a man emerged. He was probably six feet tall, with broad shoulders and a well-muscled chest and arms. He wore jeans, work boots, and a flannel shirt with sleeves rolled up to the elbows. The sound of his steps was like gunshots as he stomped toward me with fire in his eyes.

"What are you doing on my land?" he growled.

I hit the side of my truck as I instinctively took a step back. Rage was an emotion I recognized on sight. Every fiber of my being was screaming at me to run. My mother had trained me to look for rage and get out immediately if I ever saw it brewing and, if I couldn't leave, to never show my fear. Things got dangerous when people were this angry. I forced my body to stay still. I straightened my spine, pulling myself up to my full height, and stepped away from the truck.

"Mr. Burrows? My name's Megan Miller. I'm helping the sheriff with an investigation." I was proud of how steady my voice sounded to my ears.

He lurched to a stop about ten paces away, crossed his arms, and glared at me. "What sort of investigation?"

"I'm looking into the death of Avery McGlynn."

His eyes narrowed. "What do you need to know?"

I cleared my throat and shifted my weight until it was balanced evenly between my feet so I could get away quickly if I needed to. "When did you last see her?"

"Six days ago." His answer was short and to the point, his words coming out between gritted teeth.

"Okay… what was your last interaction like?"

"Tense."

I kept my face impassive. "Could you expand on that?"

"Avery stole one of my hives." He shifted an inch forward. "She snuck onto my property in the middle of the night and took off with one of the boxes."

I blinked. I wasn't sure what I'd been expecting, but it wasn't that. "Did you catch her in the act?"

"No."

"Then how do you know she did it?"

He jerked his head toward his house. "I have a Ring cam."

"Did you report it to the police?" I asked.

"No."

I held back an exasperated sigh. Travis was the least forthcoming individual I had ever spoken to. In comparison, Russell had been downright cheery.

"Can I look at your shoes?" I asked.

Travis's mouth opened to respond, but he snapped it shut as a black SUV pulled into the driveway and a woman with strawberry-blond hair stepped out. She had a wide smile and wore a white-and-blue sundress. She bent into the back seat and stood back up with a toddler, who had the same strawberry-blond hair, in her arms.

Travis's head swiveled between them and me, his eyes widening. He stepped between us, blocking my view. "Get in the house."

The woman's smile vanished, and she nodded. She scurried away. The toddler stared at me, wide-eyed, over the woman's shoulder. I peered over Travis's shoulder at them. He shifted forward, obstructing my view again.

"Who are you representing when you ask all these questions? You said you were here on behalf of the sheriff, but I don't see a badge."

"I work for city council. They tasked—"

He snorted. "City council? Are you really here for them or for the Wardens?"

I clamped my mouth shut. *How does he know about the Wardens?* I made my expression blank. "I am a liaison between the two."

"Then no."

I blinked. "No, what?"

"To seeing my shoes."

My world tilted under me. There was something happening here, and I didn't know what it was. He had been aggressive out the gate. Diana had said he had a temper, but this felt like more than that. It felt personal for some reason.

What's his problem with me? What should I do next—continue the questions? I had watched a ton of *Law and Order* episodes on TV over the years, so I opted to go with one of the standard questions next.

"Where were you Friday between ten p.m. and midnight?"

He scoffed again. "You expect me to believe you care about my alibi? Really?"

What is going on? I studied him. His body was practically

vibrating with rage, but under that, he looked almost frightened. "Why wouldn't I care?" I asked.

He stepped forward. He was so close, his reddened face and broad shoulders were all I could see. *How did he get so close?* I forced myself to stand still. He was trying to bully me, and flinching would only spur him on.

"You don't think I know how you witches view us mutts?" He spat the word *mutts*. "You're always trying to pin things on us."

"Just… tell me where you were, and I'll get out of your hair."

"I was with my pack." He cracked his neck.

My mouth was dry. I swallowed past it. "Could I speak with them to confirm?"

"Why? So you can blame them too?" He shook his head, and his voice rose. "You need to leave."

He was even closer now. With each word, he had inched forward. He loomed over me almost as if he'd gotten bigger since I had arrived.

I glanced down at his clenched fists and took an involuntary step backward. "If you didn't—"

Travis reached for me. "I'm done talking. Leave. Now."

My heart skipped a beat. Diana's warning to be cautious replayed in my mind. I stumbled backward into my truck door. A single word, willed with panic-fueled magic, tumbled out of my mouth. "Sleep!"

Travis wavered on his feet. He stared at me for a second, fear warring with exhaustion. The fatigue won. He tumbled forward. I lunged toward him and caught him before he fell on his face. My muscles protested under the sudden weight. Travis wasn't a small guy, and while I was not weak, I wouldn't be able to hold him up for long. I lowered him to the ground as gently as I could. He curled onto his side, his arm acting as a pillow under his head.

I stared down at him. In sleep, he seemed peaceful. His

angry expression had softened. I glanced between him and the house. The door was closed, and no one was looking out.

"This is a bad idea," I murmured as I scurried toward his feet.

I picked up his foot and checked the sole. The shoe was the right size, but the tread was completely different. *He could have been wearing different shoes.* I set his foot down gently and backed away.

After I climbed into my truck, I stared at him for a beat longer. I didn't know how long the sleep spell would last, and even though he'd acted threatening toward me, I didn't want him to get hurt by something, or someone, coming across him while he was unconscious. I put my truck in reverse and backed a few feet away down the driveway. When I was halfway down, I paused and honked the horn. I waited until the woman appeared in the doorway of the house. She stared at me. I gave her an apologetic smile then backed out the rest of the way off their property. While I wasn't sure if the woman would be strong enough to carry him, she would at least be able to make sure he stayed safe.

I stopped a few blocks away and leaned back in my seat with my eyes closed. "Well, that could have gone better."

I replayed the conversation. He'd been more aggressive than I had anticipated. *Mutts. Pack. Was that a werewolf?*

I straightened and shifted my truck into drive. There was still a giant question mark next to Travis's name. I would definitely need some advice from my coven on how to proceed on that front. I had just stumbled into the middle of werewolf–witch hostilities that I was unaware of. This made my job a whole lot more complicated.

My day just got more interesting. You guys OK with meeting me for lunch?

Dani:
Slice of Life?

Kim:
Abby just put blondies back on the menu.

Heather:
Is that a yes to Slice of Life?

Kim:
How is that even a question? It's the superior dessert.

I'll meet you guys there in 30.

Hopefully, my coven mates would know how to nip the situation with Travis in the bud before tensions escalated any further. I didn't know how many people were in his pack, but I was enjoying being a bit more social, and I didn't want to create a bunch of enemies over what I was hoping was a simple misunderstanding.

CHAPTER 9

Even well past the lunch rush, the Slice of Life Diner was half full. My head jerked up, and I stared straight ahead as I walked through the room to the counter along the back wall. Ever since Abby and Willow had teamed up to run the place, it had been the most popular restaurant in all of Point Pleasant. People came from the surrounding areas to eat food from their ever-evolving menu. I was still getting used to being around this many people. Fortunately the restaurant was open and airy, which made the space feel less claustrophobic with all the people gathered inside. The walls were covered in photos. The theme this month was celebration, so each one was of a celebration that had taken place around the town, with photos from every decade. Black-and-white pictures hung next to the bright, colorful ones from the eighties. Every single one had groups of smiling faces. I allowed myself to relax and look at the photos as I walked past them. It was hard not to smile as my gaze slid from photo to photo.

I waved to Kim and Dani, who were already seated at our regular booth in the back, before stepping up to the counter to give them my order. I glanced up at the menu. On one side was Eats, a list of all their current entrée specials, and on the other side Treats, a list of their desserts. Milkshakes with pie crumbled into the mix were their specialty. My mouth watered at the thought of a Peanut-Butter-Pie Milkshake.

"What will it be?" Abby wore a white chef's coat. Her pixie cut had recently been dyed bright pink, and it stuck out from her head at whimsical angles.

"The usual." My regular order was their roast beef stew with a chunk of fresh baked bread. "And the Peanut-Butter-Pie Milkshake."

"One of these days, you're going to try something new." Abby grinned.

I returned her smile. "As soon as the usual stops tasting so delicious."

As I was paying, Heather stepped up behind me to put in her order. She squeezed my shoulder as I passed. "I'll meet you at the table," she said.

I wound my way through the room. Dani stood and pulled me into a hug before I claimed the seat next to Kim. I bumped Kim lightly with my shoulder. "Thanks for having your kids come over this morning."

"They'll be over every morning until your investigation is done," Kim said.

My stomach tightened. "Oh, they don't have—"

Kim turned her head toward me and gave me a hard stare. "Don't start with that. You need the help. Plus, I don't think I could convince Lindsey not to even if I wanted to. She was over the moon about getting to work with animals. Don't take that away from her because you've got some guilt complex over accepting aid."

Before I could respond, Heather was sliding into the booth across from me, distracting the table from my flushed face. Kim knew me too well. There were days when I appreciated having a best friend who called me on my behavior.

This was one of the rare days when I wished for a gentler approach, but I needed her brutal honesty.

Heather unloaded the tray of food, sliding a salmon burger with sweet potato fries in front of Dani, a salad heaped with feta, strawberries, and diced chicken in front of Kim, and a beef stew in front of me. I raised an eyebrow at Heather when all she grabbed from the tray for herself was a root beer.

She slumped into her seat and sipped her drink. "I had planned on eating lunch with you guys, but I'm working on a new recipe at the café for morning glory muffins. I haven't quite got the pineapple-to-coconut ratio right yet, which means many rounds of taste testing. I'm stuffed."

"I volunteer myself to taste test the next batch," Dani said.

"You say that, but will you be as willing three batches from now?" Heather fidgeted with the end of her braid. "I'm up to batch fourteen. I'm close to throwing in the towel."

I flashed Heather a reassuring smile. "They can't be that bad. You're a fantastic cook."

Heather leaned her head back. "They're not. Becca says every batch has been fine, but I don't want to serve them until they meet my standards." She sighed. "Enough about my perfectionist woes. How's the investigation going? How’s it been working with Victor?" She waggled her eyebrows at me.

A flush crept up the back of my neck, and my back stiffened. Clearing my throat, I straightened in my seat, a polite smile crossing my lips. Even around my coven, my body didn't let me show my vulnerabilities—the moment I became anxious, I took on an air of confidence.

I updated them on how my day had gone so far, glossing over my concerns about what Miranda could be doing to Victor’s head. I didn’t need to derail the conversation when there was nothing we could do about it. "I'm not sure exactly what Travis is, but he was really worked up over the fact that I work with the Wardens. He said something about them viewing him as a mutt and that I wouldn't believe his alibi because he was with his pack. I'm figuring... werewolf maybe? They exist, right? Either way, he tried to grab me. I panicked and may have cast a sleeping spell on him in his driveway."

My coven sat in a stunned silence.

Kim was the first to talk. "The witch community has been so insular here that I've honestly never put much thought into what other supernaturals might be lurking about."

"I wish there was a handbook on paranormal relations," Dani said.

"Have you thought about contacting the Retirees?" Heather asked. The Retirees were a group of witches who had lived in Point Pleasant my entire life. They'd mentored almost everyone at the table before they took off on a road trip across the US in a Winnebago. "They've probably encountered a lot more groups than we have. Plus, they'll probably be a bit more forthcoming than the Wardens. Can you picture Miranda admitting there's tension between them and another group?"

I nodded along and pulled out my phone. I opened up the text thread with the Retirees, who had been sending us photos of their adventures. They'd popped back into town for a few days for Dani's wedding before heading out again. The last update, which they'd sent two days ago, was that they were on their way to see the Grand Canyon.

> Hey, guys! I'm having an odd first week in my new liaison position. I interviewed someone who I think is a wolf on the weekends, and he got all bent out of shape about me working for the Wardens. Do you know anything about friction between them and other groups?

I shoved my phone into my pocket so I wouldn't stare at it. "Sent."

"What are you planning on doing next?" Kim asked.

I grabbed the list they'd put together for me during our last coven meeting. "I could actually use your help on that front. The friends I've interviewed didn't know what had been going on with Avery lately. And I couldn't find any mention of family online. But to be honest, I don't even know if she would have a family. Do dryads have kids the same way we do? All I know about them is that they're some sort of tree spirit. How long do they live? I'm kind of spiraling."

"It sounds like you need to confirm Travis's alibi," Heather said.

I jotted that down.

"You should think about using an illusion spell so he doesn't recognize you," Kim suggested.

"Good idea." I noted that down.

"It might be worth interviewing people at the campaign headquarters." Dani tapped her fingers on the table. "From the sound of things, Avery changed recently. The only new thing you've found so far is her involvement in the campaign. It feels like there's something going on there."

I added *interview campaign manager* to the list. "I've also been thinking I need to go back out to the crime scene. I wasn't able to get too close because of how aggressive the bees were. I'm hoping they've calmed down enough that I can take a look around."

Kim rolled her shoulders. "I'll go with you."

"Me too," Dani said.

"A group activity? Count me in." Heather smiled. "So long as it can wait an hour. Becca's closing tonight, but I'll need to cover her for a bit while she takes her lunch break."

"That's fine. I'll interview the campaign manager first, and then we can meet out there." I shifted in my seat as an uncomfortable thought crossed my mind. "I just hope they're not secretly supernatural too."

Heather cocked her head. "Is there a way to check?"

"Not to my knowledge," Kim said.

I grinned as an idea began to form. "Not yet. But we could craft a spell to do it."

Dani grabbed her purse and pulled out a notebook. "We could modify a tracking spell."

Kim nodded. "Or a variation of a true-sight spell."

The muscles in my legs twitched under the table. Divination magic was not my strong suit, and both those spells relied on a strong divination background. While I might be able to pull it off, I wouldn't be able to easily do it on the fly. Not without eating an absurd amount of jerky to keep my energy levels up. *It's too bad an enchantment spell couldn't work as the base. Or a transformation—*

My head jerked up. A transformation spell would work. While most witches relied on divination magic to heighten their senses, Betty, one of the Retirees, had taught me a variation that changed the body instead.

"What about a transformation spell? Something that changes my eyes?"

Kim grabbed the notebook from Dani. "That could work."

She wrote down the base spell that she knew and, in the margins, a few ideas for ways to modify it. Then she handed the journal off to me. I modified the spell to the way I'd been taught it and scribbled a few of my ideas under hers. I handed the notebook off to Dani next. We passed it around, adding and crossing things out, as the idea took shape. The only issue was maintaining the spell.

"How are we supposed to maintain it long enough for it to be useful?" I asked.

Heather perked up. "Why don't you tie it to an object?"

"It would have to be something that goes over my eyes, and I don't wear glasses. Sunglasses could work, maybe." I pursed my lips and thought it through. It was late spring, but the days still weren't particularly long. After dark, if I needed to check to see if someone was supernatural, it would look very strange for me to whip out a pair of sunglasses.

Heather leaned down and snaked her purse from under the table. She rummaged inside it and pulled out a black compact. "Eye shadow?"

I nodded. "That could work."

She pulled the packaging off and dropped the container into my hand. "I'll donate it to the cause."

I set the compact down and pulled the notebook back toward me. I jotted down a few more lines to modify the spell so as to attach to an object instead of changing me directly. I quickly reconciled our notes into a single, more legible spell and then slid the page back across the table to Dani. Both she and Kim read through it. They handed it back with a nod.

"All right, let's give this a shot," I said.

I clasped the eye shadow in one hand and muttered the words of the spell. My magic had always looked like rose petals. I assumed that was because enchantment magic was my specialty and flowers were almost always a surefire way to impact someone's mood. I reached out and grabbed onto the stream of petals. They had no weight, but somehow, I could still sense their energy between my fingers. I ran my fingers together like I was rolling a ball of dough into a line. The petals swirled closer and closer together until they looked like a red thread. I tied the thread around the compact and continued muttering the spell until it flashed and the magic sank into the container.

"Did it work?" As the only nonwitch at the table, Heather couldn't see what I had just done.

"I think so." I flipped the container open. The eye shadow was a brilliant green. It complemented Heather's red hair. On me, it would look a little bright.

I held up my phone to use the camera app and carefully spread a little of the makeup on my eyelids. It didn't take long for the spell to take hold of me. Across the table, Dani and Kim lit up like beacons while Heather remained her normal self. I glanced out over the Slice of Life Diner. Everyone looked normal except for Abby. She had a subtle glow that was different from Dani and Kim's. It was so muted it barely registered. She had never reacted to us casting spells in her presence. I doubted she was a witch, but she was something. I filed that information away and swept my gaze around the room again. Only Dani, Kim, and Abby had taken on a glow.

"It worked." I smiled. "Now I feel a whole lot more confident interviewing the campaign manager."

We chatted a few more minutes and then split up to go tackle our various duties for the evening. Heather headed back to the Bizzy Bean so Becca could take her lunch break. Kim went back home. She worked remotely as a medical bill coder. Dani took off for a home inspection—she worked as an independent claims adjuster, and there was a roof leak that needed her expert eye.

I wandered outside last, my eyes flicking over the people on the street as I made my way to my truck. Almost everyone looked normal, but here or there, I noticed a few people shimmering with different types of energy. I kept my expression impassive. There were a lot more supernaturally touched people in our community than I had thought. This was going to be interesting.

CHAPTER 10

Amanda Yu's campaign office was only a few blocks away from the Slice of Life Diner. She rented office space over a yarn store. I ended up leaving my truck there and walking over. The stairs creaked under me as I strode up them. There were four doors off the landing, two leading to apartments and the other two leading to office space.

The door to Amanda's office was wide open, and a man's raised voice escaped it. "Four more missing? You've got to be kidding me. Where were these ones located?"

I inched forward. The responding voice was muffled and belonged to someone who was facing away from the door and spoke in an even, measured tone. I peeked around the corner. The office was a large open space with desks crammed into every corner. In the back were two doors, one leading to an even smaller office and the other to a bathroom. Potted plants lined every windowsill, giving the room an inviting feel despite the clutter. Most of the desks were occupied by people who were busily typing away. In the center of the room, Amanda Yu's campaign manager, Todd Fitzgerald, whom I recognized from her website, was talking to one of the volunteers. Todd went by TJ. I wasn't sure what the J stood for. He was a bit taller than me, with narrow shoulders. He wore a blue suit, minus the jacket, and the sleeves of his white shirt were rolled up. His close-cropped hair was mussed as if he had run his fingers through it one too many times. In his online photo, he had a friendly smile and looked like the definition of approachable, but there in the office, his face was pulled into a scowl. Everyone in the room appeared to be as they were, without a single supernatural in sight.

TJ pinched the bridge of his nose. "All right. Let's just get new ones out, then. Replace the missing signs on the corners of Fourth and Main, and Jefferson and Marine View. The other two are lost causes at this point. Check with the mosaic place again. Mr. Porter seemed willing to put them up last time we spoke. Also make another pass at the Slice of Life Diner and the Bizzy Bean. It's rare to get signs up at either place, but they're bedrocks. If we get them up there, we're almost guaranteed to win. Try Abby, not Willow. She's the more civic-minded of the two. Try talking up Amanda's goal to rezone that area off of Ninety-Fourth so it can be transformed into a women's shelter. She'll eat that up. Oh, and don't bother Mr. Bennett again. He's more likely to throw his lot in if he feels we're respecting his wishes to stay out of things. But given his history, there's no way he'll stay out of it through election day. He's way too opinionated for that. Got it?"

My mind whirled as the volunteer he was talking to nodded and grabbed a stack of campaign signs. I could understand why Fitzgerald was considered an effective campaign manager for local politics. He seemed to know Point Pleasant inside and out. The volunteer ducked past me and scurried away down the stairs to fulfill their marching orders.

TJ glanced over at me. His scowl disappeared and was replaced with the friendly smile from the website. "Sorry about that. The office is a bit chaotic right now. We're dealing with a menace who has been vandalizing and stealing our signs all over town. It's probably a group of kids, based on the crude imagery. How can I be of assistance to you today, Miss Miller?"

I blinked. *How does he know my name?*

His smile widened. "Are you here on personal business or in your official role as a consultant for the city council?"

Of course he would know about me. He probably has headshots of all the people who work for the city council tucked away somewhere. I pulled my shoulders back and walked into the room. "Official business, unfortunately. I'm assisting with the investigation into Avery McGlynn's death."

His smile fell. "Let's take this to my office."

I followed him back. TJ's office wasn't much bigger than a closet. He had enough space for his desk, a chair and a single filing cabinet.

He cleared extra signs off the seat opposite his and motioned for me to sit. "You said Avery McGlynn?"

I nodded.

He spun to his computer and typed her name in. His head dropped when her volunteer photo came up on his screen. "I knew her name sounded familiar. I remember her now. What can I do to help?"

"I understand she was a volunteer here. I was wondering if anything stood out to you about her interactions with you or any of the other volunteers."

He shook his head. "I wish I could be of more help. I remember her signing up. It looks like she went through orientation a week later but then never came back."

"Did anyone follow up with her?"

"We sent a few follow-up text messages, but she never

responded." He leaned back in his chair and folded his hands over his stomach. "It's honestly not that unusual. Campaigns are more work than most people think. Well, I should say good campaigns. After people find out the type of stuff they would actually have to do and the reality of talking to so many strangers sinks in, half are no-shows. And after that, only about a third continue past the first few weeks with any consistency. Volunteering is noble, but it is a big ask with how busy people's lives can be."

"Was she closer to some of the volunteers than others?" I asked.

He tilted his head back. "I don't think so. What I remember is she was very enthusiastic when she first signed up. I really thought she was going to be a longtimer. But at the orientation, she was distracted and didn't really talk to the others. I don't even remember when she left. I don't recall her saying goodbye."

"Do you remember what she was most excited about?"

He gave me a well-practiced bashful smile. "Most people don't realize how important local politics can be. They actually have a huge impact on people's lives. But it's hard to get excited about the more unsexy topics, like zoning. That's the cornerstone of Amanda's campaign. Avery was the first person I've seen who actually got as passionate about zoning as Amanda does. She was thrilled about there being more public parks. Steven's been trying to revitalize the downtown, but there've been snags here and there. To make a place as beautiful as it can be, you need more parks. More green spaces where people can enjoy being outside. It's Amanda's goal to make it so you're within three or four blocks of a park at all times. Even small greenbelts have an impact on community happiness scores and air quality."

"Parks?"

"Yeah. Haven't you noticed that once you leave the boardwalk area, there are only about three parks in all of Point

Pleasant? Especially when you get into the suburbs. And it's not that there isn't land available. They're just zoned wrong, so they can't be turned into places where families can gather."

I smiled at him. Now that he mentioned it, I couldn't think of a single park in town. I knew there had to be some, but for the life of me, I couldn't picture them. "It seems like Avery and Amanda aren't the only ones passionate about zoning."

He shrugged. "I read up on the issues important to my clients. It's hard not to have them become important to me, too, when I talk about them so often. It's one of the things I really love about local politics and why I won't take on any campaigns past county level. I like to believe my clients are running because they want to make their communities better. And you can have a much bigger impact when you're building from the ground up than from the top down. It allows you to take the individual into account instead of just the statistics of a state or national campaign."

I studied him. I wasn't sure what to make of him. He seemed sincere, but it was his job to read as trustworthy. Nothing he said tripped any red flags in my mind. I wondered why Avery had volunteered but then dropped out early.

"When was the orientation?" I asked.

"We have one every week, but Avery went to the one four weeks ago."

Four weeks. It lines up with her cutting out Jessica. What happened four weeks ago? Whatever it was had stopped her from continuing on as a volunteer. But honestly, I wasn't sure how much to focus on that.

"Was there anything else?" he asked.

I pushed myself to my feet and shook his hand. "I think that's it. If you think of anything else important, please call me."

He took down my number and then walked me out. I

shuffled down the stairs and made my way back to my truck. The campaign had been a dead end. Hopefully, my trek out to Avery's apiary with my coven would prove more useful. I drove back to my own farm on autopilot to collect Gertie for the ride out.

CHAPTER 11

I swayed with Gertie as she ambled down the dirt road toward Dani's car. The sun hung low in the sky, its rays at that awkward angle that felt like no matter where I looked, I was staring directly into the sun. I squinted ahead of me as I guided Gertie up to my coven mates' vehicles, which were parked at the end of the road. Dani's car sat nestled next to a massive red Polaris ATV. As I approached, the lights to Dani's car turned off, and she and Heather got out. I came to a stop next to them. Heather absentmindedly stroked Gertie's nose as she admired the ATV.

Dani whistled and walked around it. "When did you get this?"

Kim shrugged a single shoulder. "A few weeks back. I got it for Conner. He's been thrilled about all the outdoor activities he can do with it."

Dani grinned and patted the hood. "It would be great for getting to remote camping spots. I've been meaning to go camping with Chris this summer. It's been years since I've done that."

"We should do a group camping trip before Grace takes

off for school." Heather hopped up into the front seat. "Shotgun!"

Kim clambered up into the driver's seat. "Sounds good to me."

"Me too," I said.

Dani claimed the last spot in the ATV. "I'm game. I'll figure out scheduling with Grace and Chris when I get home."

I guided Gertie with my knees into the trees. "Avery's house is this way."

The ATV's engine growled behind me as we made our way through the woods. I led them along the winding game trail until it opened up at the meadow. Gertie ground to a halt at the fence and snorted her displeasure. I patted her shoulder and slipped off her back.

"You can stay here, girl," I murmured into her ear.

Kim parked the ATV as close to the fence as she could get, and my coven climbed down to join me.

Heather stared, wide-eyed, at the meadow. "This place is giving me some *Sleeping Beauty* vibes."

"Where did you want to start?" Dani asked.

I opened the gate and ushered them toward the redbrick cottage. "I wasn't able to get close to the beehives last time I was here. And I only made it through about half the house before I got distracted by a neighbor."

"The home, then?" Kim asked.

I nodded and led them inside. We gave the hives a wide berth in case the bees came out again. The hives were quiet as we slipped in through the front door. The room was exactly as I'd left it—cluttered, but giving the impression that everything had its place.

"I was looking over the paperwork on the table when I was interrupted," I said.

"I'll help you finish looking through it," Heather volunteered.

Dani strode toward the stairs. "I'll take the bedroom loft."

"I've got the bathroom," Kim said.

We split up and began to search. I pawed through the stacks I had previously gone through, to make sure I hadn't missed anything, and then moved on to the less organized stacks of paperwork. Mail, interspersed with sheet music and random flyers, took up a large section of the counter. I shuffled the papers into one large stack then split it with Heather to go through. I leaned back against the counter and flipped through the assortment of papers. My hands stilled when I came across unsigned eviction paperwork.

I pulled it out and then quickly flipped through the rest of the stack before setting everything else aside. Every section of the paperwork had been filled out except for the signature and dates. I couldn't tell if this was new or if it had been sitting on the counter for a while. But in either case, Avery was prepared to start the eviction process for Diana. She was planning on kicking her out of her cabin. My breath caught in my throat as I recalled the letter I'd found in Diana's trash, begging Avery not to go through with something. *Is this what Diana was talking about—losing her home?*

I held up the paperwork. "I think I may have just found the motive."

Dani poked her head over the railing. "What is it?"

"Avery was going to evict Diana."

"I think I found an even better one." Heather held up a document, her eyes gleaming.

I cocked my head as she gave it to me to read.

"Avery was changing her will," Heather said as I read through the document. "She hadn't finished yet. It's not signed. But she was going to leave a rather sizable estate to Jessica, and she was changing it to leave the money to a few local charities instead."

Dani walked down the stairs and took the papers from me once I was done reading. "That's a lot of money."

"Did you find anything in the bedroom?" I asked.

Dani shook her head as she continued reading. "And a lot of land. Someone would kill for that."

Kim emerged from the bathroom. "Nothing in here either. How much money are we talking about?"

Dani handed off the paperwork, and Kim's eyes widened. It wasn't the kind of money that made a person independently wealthy, but it was life-changing. "Yeah. That's a motive."

I snapped photos of the paperwork and then slipped it into a plastic bag Kim had brought from her house. We took one last pass around the house and then went outside to take a closer look at the crime scene. The bees were still in their hives. A quiet buzzing seeped out of them as we crept closer. We fanned out to cover more ground. My eyes were glued to the ground as I padded across the grass.

"Huh. I wonder what that is," Dani said off to my left.

I looked up. She was pointing at something that hung from twine underneath the hive. I studied it as I inched closer. It almost looked like a flower from a distance, but as I got closer, it took shape. It had four petallike points and an overlapping circle. I squinted at it as I crouched next to the hive. The thing almost looked like a witch's knot but was more irregular in shape. The wood was blackened, and there was a tarry substance on the joints. There was something familiar about the shape, but I couldn't place it.

I reached forward, and the buzzing near my head intensified. I glanced at the hive opening just in time to see a swarm of bees erupt out of it. They descended around me as I scrambled backward on my hands. My mouth opened to scream. The sound caught in my throat as something crashed loudly behind me. I whipped my head around, trying to find the source of the sound, as I continued to scramble backward. Kim was yelling. Heather and Dani's voices joined the mix. A wall of magic snapped into place between me and the hive. Unfortunately, half the swarm had already reached me. I winced as the first bee stung my throat.

Gertie plowed past me and threw her body between me and the bees. She swung her head and tail this way and that, forcing them out of the air. I surged to my feet and hugged Gertie's side, and she turned in place, positioning me between her and the magical wall created by Kim. Two more bees stung my exposed arms. I swatted them away as golden motes of light swirled around me. Dani was casting. I steadied my breathing and began murmuring the words to a calming spell. Kim's copper orbs circled through the air, intermingling with Dani's and my magic, as she worked to bolster our effects.

The bees fought off my will. They dove toward me. Kim's barrier expanded outward, cutting them off before any more could land on my skin.

"We need to get out of here!" Kim shouted.

I nodded and pushed on Gertie, nudging her back toward the gate. Kim, Dani, and Heather joined me, and together, we inched our way forward. I poured everything I had into pacifying the swarm, while Dani and Kim kept them at bay. I managed to get half of them to calm down enough to fly back to their hive, but the rest hounded us until the second we crossed the white picket fence, and then they turned as one and flew back.

Heather panted. "What on earth…? That was intense."

"Did you get a good look at the charm under the hive? Was it magical?" Dani asked.

I shook my head. "It looked almost like a witch's knot but was wrong somehow. I didn't get close enough to figure out what was up with it." I gestured to my eyes. Dani and Kim both still glowed under the effects of the magical eyeshadow. "And I don't know if this picks up all magic or just magical people."

Kim exhaled slowly then climbed into the driver's seat of

the ATV. "It's too much of a coincidence to ignore. I wonder who put it there."

"It looked familiar." I closed my eyes, trying to remember where I had seen hand-carved wooden figurines like them before. Moon and Mortar. They had hung over the windows. I grimaced. "I think they belong to Jessica."

That was another mark against her. It was time for a second interview.

CHAPTER 12

By the time we made it back to town, it was after dark. Moon and Mortar had closed for the day, and the idea of tracking down Jessica at her house was daunting after all the magic I'd used at the apiary. My whole body ached from the encounter, with my throat and left arm being especially sore from the bees that had landed there and stung me. We separated for the night, and I rode Gertie back home to lick my wounds and eat an entire pint of Ben & Jerry's Cherry Garcia. I was so tired I almost passed out on the couch.

The next morning, I crawled out of bed to do farm chores. Conner had overslept, but Lindsey was already in the barn, mucking out stalls, when I stumbled in twenty minutes behind schedule. The stings were raised and puffy and ached whenever my flannel shirt slid across them. I thanked Kim silently for sending her daughter my way. Twenty minutes after dawn, we parted ways. I showered quickly, inhaled half a dozen eggs for breakfast, and then headed out to confront Jessica as soon as she opened her doors for the day.

I sat in my truck across the street from her shop, peering over my steering wheel at the darkened windows. Someone was moving around inside, but the sign hadn't flipped to

Open yet. I shifted in my seat, trying to find a comfortable position. I winced as the collar of my shirt brushed up against my beestings. At exactly nine o'clock, the sign on the door flipped from Closed to Open. I typed out a brief message to my coven, letting them know what I was about to do, then grabbed my backpack and jumped out of the truck. I strode across the street.

Jessica had only made it halfway across the store by the time I stepped inside. I studied her from across the room as she turned. I had reapplied the supernatural-detecting eyeshadow in the truck. She glowed with the same type of energy as Dani and Kim, although hers was more muted. I'd already known she was a witch, but this confirmed it.

"You're here early. Looking for something in particular?" Jessica asked.

I took another step into the room. Something about the way she was standing—a little too rigid, with her shoulders rolled inward—made me think she felt uneasy. Discomfort was one of the emotions my mom had trained me to read well. It was a precursor to other, less savvy responses.

I studied her face as I spoke. "My investigation is still ongoing, and I hoped I could ask you a few more questions."

She turned fully to face me. "Of course."

I shifted my backpack on my shoulder and pulled out a few candles and a lighter. "I need to make sure I'm getting the whole truth from you, so I'm going to cast a lie-detection spell if it's all right with you."

She stiffened. Her lips pressed together into a tight, straight line. She jerked her head in acknowledgment.

I stalked around the room, placing a candle at each of the four corners and lighting them one by one. As I made the rotation, I murmured the words to the spell that would alert me if any untruths were spoken in the circle. Lastly, I fished out a piece of sodalite from my bag and handed it to Jessica. The color drained from her face as she turned it over in her hands. If she lied while holding it, the dark-blue stone would change into the bright yellow of the flames.

"Is this entirely necessary?" she asked.

"Unfortunately." I stepped away from her and pointed at the wooden figurine over the window. "What is this?"

Jessica glanced at it. "A protective charm. Although these haven't been activated yet."

"Are they used for anything else?"

"No."

"I saw one like this at the apiary, under the hives."

Jessica nodded. "I put some there about a year ago. I'm not the most powerful witch. They only last about a month before I have to recast the spell. I anoint them in myrrh oil. After Avery stopped talking to me, I didn't go back out to reactivate them. They're probably dead by now."

My brow furrowed as I studied her. *So why were the bees so aggressive? There has to have been something magic involved. My magic barely calmed them at all. But the stone's still blue. She isn't lying.*

"Did you want me to demonstrate activating one so you can look at the protective spell yourself? It's harmless."

"Sure," I said.

Jessica walked to the counter in the back and grabbed a vial of dark-brown liquid from underneath. She carried it over to the wooden carvings and tugged one off its hook. As she spoke the words to the spell, loudly enough for me to hear, she rubbed a bit of the oil from the bottle onto the wood. Her magic flowed out of her fingertips. It had a metallic quality that reminded me of Kim's magic and gave the oil a silver sheen. The darkness of the oil and the silver of Jessica's magic seeped into the wood until the carving gently glowed. I stared at it in her hands, relaxing my eyes until I could see the individual threads of the spell that she had wrapped around the wood. Her words spoke of protection, and the threads were all abjuration magic in origin. Abjuration spells focused on shielding things from harm. It was saying *no* to something with magic. No, a ghost can't come in here. No, that harmful spell cannot be cast. Abjuration magic didn't cause things to happen, it prevented them. Jessica's spell wasn't particularly powerful, but it seemed designed to repel negative energies.

She hung the protective charm up and returned to her position in the middle of the room. "As you can see, a simple protection spell. Is that what this was all about?"

"Half of it. I did have another question for you."

"Okay. I've got nothing to hide." Jessica held her hands out at her sides. "Ask away."

The stone was still dark in her hand.

I cocked my head. “If you've got nothing to hide, why are you so nervous?”

“You work for the Wardens. Why wouldn't I be nervous?”

I would need to find a way to clarify my role with the community. The guilt by association was making questioning people difficult. I cleared my throat and continued the interview. "Did you know that Avery was planning on changing her will?"

"What will?" Jessica squinted at me. "Avery had a will?"

"Please, just answer the question. Did you know Avery was planning on changing her will?" I stared at the stone in her hands. My whole body was tense, waiting for her response.

"No. I didn't even know she had one. Why does that matter?" The stone stayed blue.

"In the original will, you inherited everything."

"Everything?" Jessica spluttered. "So, like, her cottage and the apiary? Why would she do that?" Her shoulders dropped, and she lowered her head, her hair hiding her face. "Because of Liam. She loves… loved my son. He's heartbroken about her death. I finally told him last night. He's never lost someone before, and it took him some time to realize it was final. What is she doing instead?"

"She was changing it to a local charity."

Jessica nodded. "That's good. There's a lot of worthy causes around here."

"She hadn't changed it yet."

Jessica's head jerked up, surprise clear on her face. "You think—I didn't know. I would never hurt someone over money. Especially not a friend. I had nothing to do with her death. I promise. I still thought we were going to reconnect, you know? We've been friends since high school. I thought... I thought this was going to be temporary and then I would have my friend back. And now she's gone." Her voice broke on the word *gone.* Jessica started sobbing.

I didn't know what to say to that. The stone was still blue in her hands—everything she said was true. She didn't have anything to do with Avery's death. My stomach roiled as I shuffled around the room, collecting the candles. Jessica had just lost a friend and then had to deal with me questioning her.

How does anyone do this? Interviewing grieving people is awful. I blew out the last candle and then crossed the room to collect the stone from Jessica. She gave it back without a word.

"I'm sorry for your loss."

Jessica wiped her eyes. "I wish there was something I could do to help. It's so frustrating not knowing anything. I just have the random rumors I've been hearing from around town. Her verbal sparring match with Travis. That border dispute with her neighbor. It's all just useless gossip."

Border dispute? I filed that information away for later. Russell had reacted badly to the sight of a bee, but he might have been able to overcome that fear if Avery was encroaching on his land or vice versa. Cattle needed an awful lot of space to roam.

"You've been more helpful than you know," I said.

We talked for a few more minutes about Avery. By the time I left, Jessica didn't seem as upset about my questions. She understood how she'd ended up a suspect. At least she was a pragmatic person. I mentally took her off the list and added Russell back on it. As I slid behind the wheel of my truck, my phone chirped in my pocket. I pulled it out and stared at the message.

> **Steven Bishop:**
> Your presence is being requested at City Hall. Please come over as soon as you can this morning.

CHAPTER 13

I went straight to City Hall. The building was no less intimidating than it had been during my last visit. As I sat in my truck, I considered delaying my visit. A time hadn't been specified. But my mom had taught me to always do the hard thing first. If I got the City Hall meeting out of the way early, it wouldn't be looming over my morning like a dark cloud. As much as I would have liked to dawdle and go get coffee first, I knew if this went bad, I would need the pick-me-up afterward.

I opened the front door of City Hall and stepped into a busy lobby. A cacophony of voices washed over me, making my heart clench. Swallowing past the tightness of my throat, I strode through the room with my head held high. I added an extra little stomp to my step so people moved out of my way instead of the other way around. I was most of the way across the room when a cluster of people in front of me didn't break up fast enough. I stumbled to a stop and bumped into a man in a gray suit.

"Sorry," I mumbled as I stepped around him and wound my way through the crowd.

I only half listened to their voices as I slipped through.

My palms were sweaty. My heart beat loudly in my ears. I hated being surrounded by so many people, but there was no way to get to the council rooms without walking through this knot of people. My skin prickled as I slipped past the last of them and ducked into the empty hallway beyond. With my hands in fists, I steadied my breathing and marched down the hallway to the dark wooden double doors at the end.

When I slipped into the city council meeting chamber, it was almost exactly like it had been on my first day. On one side of the room sat the councilors, separated from the rest of the room by a wooden banister. They were all dressed similarly to the first time, except this time, Helen wore a soft pink cardigan. Chris was once again positioned on the right side, and across the aisle stood Miranda.

This time, Victor stood awkwardly next to her. He was dressed in his usual Regency-style coat over high-waisted custom-tailored black pants, fitted vest, white shirt, and cravat. His white pompadour completed the look. I tore my gaze away from him as Steven Bishop cleared his throat.

Steven smiled at me. "Thank you for coming over so quickly. I know you must be busy. But now that you're here, we might as well get started." He turned his head toward Miranda. "I understand you have new information you would like to submit."

Miranda drew herself up to her full height, her head tilted back. Her jet-black hair slid past her shoulders as she stared down her too-straight nose at the council. "I do. Victor, please share your findings."

Victor tugged on his waist coat. "After a few unforeseen delays, I was able to complete the autopsy yesterday. As we suspected, the cause of death was blunt-force trauma to the head. Based on the wound pattern, I believe it was caused by the butt of a rifle."

"And...?" Miranda prompted.

Victor shuffled on his feet. "And I can conclusively say

that the victim was not human. She appears to have been some sort of tree."

Miranda smirked as the councilors murmured to each other. From my position against the back wall, I couldn't make out what they were saying, but their tone was one of alarm.

After the council members spent a few minutes conferring with one another, Arthur Miles motioned me forward. His normally deep voice came out reedier than usual. "Miss Miller, can you give us an update on your investigation? Have you determined who the culprit is yet?"

I stepped forward into the room, and all eyes turned to me. I held my face impassive so no one could see that I was quaking in my boots. Blood whooshed through my ears as I began to speak, walking them through my investigation so far. "Currently, my lead suspects are Diana Summers, a tenant Avery was in the process of evicting; Russell Bennett, a neighbor she allegedly had some sort of border dispute with; and Travis Burrow, a rival beekeeper who had a verbal altercation with her a few days before the incident."

Miranda's smile widened, and she spun back to the councilors. "Travis is a werewolf. It's widely known how aggressive they can be. This should be on my desk."

"Hold up," Chris interjected. "It doesn't matter how many of the suspects are supernatural. The killer could still be human, and if that's the case, that is my jurisdiction. It's already muddying the waters having Megan take the lead on this. If the investigator's not even an employee of the city or on retainer with our sheriff's department, the likelihood of the charges holding up in court is zero. If it isn't what Miss Blackwood thinks, a killer could walk free. I doubt she can say the same if Megan continues to work the case. We agreed that Megan's job was to identify the killer. She hasn't done that yet."

Edgar nodded along, while the other councilors looked thoughtful.

Steven sighed and sagged into his seat. "The information has been presented. Does anyone wish to put forth a motion that the matter be formally reopened?"

The silence was deafening. The council members sat quietly as the seconds dragged on. After almost a full minute, Steven nodded. "It looks like the matter will remain closed. Megan, please continue with your investigation. We look forward to hearing another update by the end of the week."

Miranda narrowed her eyes and spun away from the room. Victor wavered in place before trudging after her. Chris and I followed a few steps behind them.

"The next item of business is the campaign signs. My office has received a few complaints that they've been particularly obnoxious this cycle." Steven's voice droned on. "There are members of the community asking for stronger guidelines on their placement."

"I've never been a fan of dictating what does or does not happen on private property. Yard signs aren't illegal," Nicholas said.

Before I could hear the next person chime in on the yard-sign drama, Chris closed the door behind us. He let out a breath and squeezed my shoulder. "You're doing great. If you need any help or suggestions, you've got my number."

"Thanks." I gave him a tight-lipped smile.

He meant well, but I wasn't sure what I'd done so far to earn his praise. I was three days into my investigation and no closer to solving the case than I had been when I first went to the morgue.

We made our way out of the building. Victor was still waiting on the sidewalk when we emerged. Chris waved and lumbered over to his SUV. I stopped next to Victor and glanced around to make sure we weren't being observed. There were a few people nearby, so I quickly mumbled the words to an illusion spell that would disguise our conversation.

He cocked an eyebrow. "I've seen Dani do that a few times. Miranda said you're all… the same type."

"Witches," I confirmed.

His eyes widened, and he dropped his voice to a whisper. "Are we supposed to talk about that out in the open? I'm still new to all this."

"I… I cast an illusion spell. If anyone were to listen in, they would think we were talking about the weather."

Victor chuckled. "I'm not sure whether I should be offended. If I was going to talk to you about anything, it would be a lot more interesting than the weather."

I flushed. "I couldn't think of anything better on short notice. But I'll keep that in mind in case we need to talk like this in the future. How are you doing with all the revelations that have been dumped on you the past few days?"

"I was shocked at first, but now I'm—excited." He grinned at me. "I made a few of the same arguments I made with you and added a few extra to make my case. Once I convinced Miranda, as well, not to wipe my memories, it became kind of thrilling really."

The tightness in my chest loosened at those words. When I had contacted Miranda about the beehive in Avery's chest, I knew she might wipe Victor's memories. She didn't strike me as someone who wouldn't do something just because I told her not to. I didn't realize how guilty I'd been feeling about it until the weight had been lifted from my shoulders.

"What was your winning argument?" I asked.

He gripped the lapel of his coat and tilted his head up with pride. "She wasn't swayed at first, so I asked a simple question to really drive that first point home: Did she have another medical examiner lined up who could work on supernatural cases for her, or was I it? She couldn't answer, so I said that while I might not know much now, I'm a quick learner, and educating me so I can help would be a much better use of her time than wiping my memories every time I encounter something strange on my table."

"And has she taught you much yet?"

He nodded enthusiastically, his blue eyes twinkling. "She's given me a field guide to the different supernatural types. I had to swear not to share it with anyone who is unaware of the supernatural community, but it's a fascinating read. While there's technically always more I can learn about the human body, this is so much more, and so much more interesting. It's like whole new field of study has opened up to me. As they say, boredom is the death of joy, and with this book, I don't think I'll be bored again a day in my life."

"You probably already know more than I do. I don't know much about the different supernatural groups yet. I'm sort of learning on the job."

"Oh. So you don't know about...?" He blinked down at me. "Well, you'll have more time once the investigation is done. Maybe we could sit down over the book and learn together. But in the meantime, I can at least go over the dryad section with you."

The butterflies that lived in my stomach and liked to dance around whenever he gave me his full attention took flight. "I'd like that."

"The book's back at my place. How about you follow me there? I've been told I make a great grilled cheese."

At the mention of food, my stomach rumbled.

Victor's smile widened. "I'll take that as a yes. I'll meet you there."

"Sure thing. It's a date. I've got a bit of time before I have to head out to do interviews. Thanks so much for doing this with me. I mean, going over the dryad entry, not eating together. But thanks for that too. I like cheese."

It's a date? I like cheese? Did those words just come out of my mouth?

Victor's eyes crinkled at the edges as he stepped back toward the road. "I'll keep that in mind for next time."

He's just being nice. It's not actually a date.

I cleared my throat and tried to return the smile without blushing too much. If it was a date, I wouldn't know what to do. It would be embarrassing.

Who makes it to forty-two without having gone out with a guy? Me. How would I even admit that to him? "Hey, Victor, I was cursed for most of my life, so no one wanted to date me. Could you recommend a good dating book for dummies?" Oh god, I've been quiet for too long. Smile. Smile and leave.

I jerked my head toward my truck. "I'll see you there."

He chuckled and took another step back. I waved awkwardly, marched to my truck, and threw myself into the driver's seat. Once I was behind the wheel, I started mentally going through everything I still had to do that day: locate a werewolf pack, reinterview the grieving artist, and if I had time, track down Russell to ask him about the border dispute. It was going to be another long day. A packed schedule was a good reason to keep our lunch short. The less time I spent at Victor's place, the less time I would have to embarrass myself again.

CHAPTER 14

I trailed behind Victor as he strode up the stairs of the funeral home to the residence above it. Before that week, I had never been outside the public-facing portion of the building, and now I'd been inside both the medical-examination rooms at the back of the building and his private space upstairs. Each section of the house felt different from the last. Downstairs was a warm but neutral space. The exam room was sterile. But upstairs, I didn't know where to look. Once I made it the landing, the paint scheme shifted from beige to navy blue and the wood from cherry to something so dark it was almost black. Despite the palette, it had the same feeling as downstairs—warm and inviting.

Victor pointed things out as I walked behind him. "The kitchen and dining room are up ahead. The main bathroom is the first door next to it on the left, if you need to use it, and my study is down the hall. I'm not sure if you're much of a reader, but I've got quite the book collection."

My gaze lingered on the one door he didn't point out. It was ajar, and I could make out the corner of a giant four-poster bed. I jerked my head away before he could catch me staring and followed him into the kitchen. It had the same dark colors as the hallway and was lit by a chandelier with flickering lightbulbs that gave the impression of fire. He flicked on more lights until the room was well lit.

I took a seat at the counter and watched as he padded around the room, collecting supplies. The bread was fresh baked and cut into thick slices. The butter, stored in a covered serving tray, was soft.

He pulled open the fridge doors and stuck his head inside. "Do you have a cheese preference? I usually go for Havarti with a bit of smoked gouda, and prosciutto for added flavor."

My stomach rumbled.

He chuckled and held up the block of cheese. "Shall I take that as an endorsement? I also have cheddar, mozzarella, gorgonzola, and parmesan. I might be a bit of a cheese snob."

I nodded. "It sounds delicious. I'm sure I'll like whatever you make."

He got to worked hand slicing the cheese and pan-frying a few slices of prosciutto. "So, how long have you known you were a witch?"

I leaned forward on my elbows. "I was lucky. My powers came in kind of late. They didn't manifest until after my junior year of high school."

"That's a good thing?" He cocked his head. "Does taking longer to develop make them more manageable or more powerful?"

"No..." My palms began to sweat. *Why did I say I was lucky? Should I just tell him? He's going to pity me—I just know it.*

"No?"

"It's actually usually the opposite. The younger you are, the more powerful you are. Most of the time. There are exceptions. I'm decently powerful but... a late bloomer."

"Then why was it a good thing?"

"It's a family thing." I held still and stared at a spot on the wall past his shoulder.

"A family..." Victor looked up and studied me. He set the

knife down. "Did I accidentally stumble onto a personal question? I'm sorry. I've always been a fan of puzzles."

"Am I a puzzle to you?"

"No. Yes. Maybe a little?" He stepped to the side to catch my gaze, his expression earnest. "But you're a friend first. At least, I hope we're friends. I wanted to get to know you better."

My heart clenched at the word *friend*. My oldest friend was Kim, and even we had lost touch for a while, in part due to my curse and in part due to hers. Both of our lives were so much better now that the curse was broken. *Friends trust each other, don't they?*

I swallowed. "I was cursed. My whole family was."

He blinked.

My mouth was dry. I swallowed. "Once our powers came in, people tended to distrust us on sight. Sometimes more than on sight. Sometimes they just had to hear our names. It made going to school interesting. But because I was such a late bloomer, I at least got to go to school until my senior year. It was mostly a normal childhood. People just hated my mom. And I... I got to have friends for a time. I was only homeschooled for the last year. That's good, right?"

"I... I was homeschooled. Well, if you consider private tutors being homeschooled. That sounds more impressive than it really was. My parents just didn't want to have to deal with me. I was a bit too rambunctious as a kid."

"Private tutors, huh?" I smiled. "Is that where your love of learning came from?"

"You could say that." He picked the knife back up and continued slicing the cheese. "I blame public libraries. When my tutors got tired of me, they would drop me off at one. While they couldn't get me to be quiet, those librarians were gold-medal shushers."

I laughed. "So, when did you figure out you wanted to be a medical examiner? It's not something most kids dream of."

He lowered his head and stared at his hands as he put together the sandwiches. He had a hitch to his shoulder.

I straightened in my seat. I'd hit a nerve somehow. "You don't have to tell me."

He shook his head. "It only seems fair. I poked at your tragic backstory."

I sat there, silently waiting for him to continue. He was going to tell me something important. I could feel it.

"My wife was murdered."

The bottom of my stomach dropped. "I'm so sorry."

He continued looking down at his hands as he slid the sandwiches onto a heated griddle. "I was in family practice at the time. I've never felt so helpless. I'm not good at feeling helpless. I did the only thing that made sense to me at the time. I threw myself into pathology. And while I never… while I couldn't help bring her killer to justice, I continued on in her memory."

"What was her name?"

"Lillian." He looked up at me, grief swimming in his eyes. "She was the sweetest woman who ever lived. Always trying to help her community. Even those most people didn't think deserved it.. And she was just at the wrong place at the wrong time."

"Was she from around here?"

He shook his head. "I came to the US after she died."

I sat back in my seat and stared at him. He had been a fixture in the community for as long as I could remember. But I came into town so infrequently that I couldn't be sure. I racked my brain, trying to think of when I'd heard about him moving here. Her death must have happened early in their marriage.

As I continued staring at him, he glanced up at me and smiled. "What are you thinking about?"

I could feel the sides of my neck flushing. Fortunately, the lighting in the kitchen was warm enough that it would be hard to make out the blushing. "It's a delicious grilled cheese."

He raised an eyebrow.

I cleared my throat. "And I didn't realize you weren't from around here."

He shrugged and continued eating his sandwich. "I've been here so long it almost feels like growing up in London was another life. So much has changed since then."

My eyes widened. He sounded like everyone else from Point Pleasant. People in the Pacific Northwest had such a mild accent that it didn't really sound like anything to me.

"You're English? But... you don't sound English."

He nodded. "Surprising, right? When I got here, I was so focused on starting afresh that I threw myself into becoming a new person. Now my accent only comes out when I've been drinking. And even then, it's barely noticeable unless you're listening for it."

I studied him as I chewed my sandwich. My curse had made it impossible to restart anywhere. I had tried to move away once when I was in my twenties, but no one would rent to me. I could have forced the issue with magic, but knowing my dad left when my mother's spell dissipated, I couldn't stand the thought of having another fake relationship. Even if it was a business relationship with a landlord.

Victor ate the last of his sandwich and wiped his hands on a napkin before shoving his plate to the side and retrieving a book from the counter behind him. The book looked like something printed at the turn of the last century. Its green cover was worn, and the gold foil was chipped.

He handed it over to me gingerly. My fingers swept across the title. *Pacific Northwest Field Guide to the Paranormal, by Harriet Spellman.*

I flipped the book open and glanced at the glossary at the front. "I don't even know what some of these are. What does *Reanimated* even mean?"

"I'm not sure yet," Victor said.

I smiled as my eyes landed on one of the final entries.

"What are you smiling at?" he asked.

I flipped the book around and pointed at the word *Vampire.* "I guess I shouldn't be surprised. It'll be fun reading up on them. My mom had a thing for old movies, so I grew up on *Nosferatu*. Vampire movies have been some of my favorite horror movies over the years. I wonder if they're accurate."

He grunted and fiddled with his jacket. "I somehow doubt it."

I pulled the book back around and read back through the list. "I don't see werewolves listed. I was hoping to read up on them after my run-in with one the other day."

"It's probably under the *Shifter* entry. It covers a wide range of shapeshifters."

"There's more than just werewolves?"

He nodded. "I haven't read up on them in detail yet, but when I flipped through, I noticed it mentioned wererats and werebears, and it looked like there was a werecougar."

"Wow."

He tugged at the collar of his shirt then reached for the book. "We can read up on those next time. We should probably start by focusing on dryads. You still have interviews to conduct today, right?"

I instantly shifted my expression to impassive to hide my disappointment. *Have I been too awkward? Does he want me to leave already? Him trying to get me to focus isn't a bad thing. But he looks uncomfortable. Just smile and move on. It's okay. He said, "next time," so he must want me to come back.*

"Right. Yeah. I've got a few interviews."

Victor scooted his chair closer to mine and flipped to the correct page. I peered over his shoulder. There was an illustration of a woman leaning against a tree. It took a second for me to notice that the woman didn't have legs.

They had merged with the tree, and just her torso was sticking out.

"Oh, that's interesting," Victor said.

"What?" I blinked.

"One of the first documented dryads was in the central Peloponnese region of Greece. It was a female dryad connected to an oak tree. Apparently, they tend to be reclusive and don't leave their orchards often. That tracks for Avery. I hardly ever saw her in town. Since the first documented case, they've been noted around the world. Apparently *Dryad* is a general classification for tree spirits. I don't know why, but it didn't occur to me that the paranormal could also have convergent evolution."

I read through the introductory text behind him and stopped at the assertion that they were an example of convergent evolution. "What does that mean?"

"Oh, um… it's like crabs. Or trees, I guess. It's basically where species, independently of each other, evolve the same traits because that form is advantageous. There are crabs and trees in tons of different places, but they aren't actually related to each other. They evolved independently."

"Oh."

I reread the section. It made sense in a way. Where there were trees, protectors of them would be needed.

Victor barked out a laugh.

"What?" I asked.

Victor cleared his throat. "The term *dryad* stuck due to the work of Margeta Zannakos, whose work on dryad mating habits gained notoriety worldwide for its blatant inaccuracies and romanization of the species. While her work is still widely quoted, any work by her is suspect since it relied on her observations of a single dryad. Any serious academic would know that an observation pool that small could produce inaccurate results."

I chuckled. "Maybe the author should tell us how she really feels."

Victor nodded and lowered his head to continue reading. Together, we skimmed over the sections about physiology and diet. It seemed the only things dryads had in common with each other were their role as protectors of the forest and their tendency to bond with trees. Some bonded with a single tree, which almost appeared to be their partner, while others bonded with a section of forest. Most dryads also shared an ability to meld with a tree. By the time I'd finished reading through those sections, I was beginning to question how useful the book would be.

"Huh." Victor tapped the book. "It lists bonding with the tree as both a strength and a weakness. Apparently, with some variations, the death of the tree leads to the death of the dryad. They are also susceptible to diseases that impact trees. Can you imagine having a bark beetle infestation?"

I shuddered. "That doesn't sound like much of a strength."

"It looks like it's considered a strength because the dryad's lifespan is extended by their connection to the trees. The oldest recorded dryad lived almost a thousand years, although it looks like most live between two hundred and three hundred years."

I skimmed through the strengths section and stopped when I came across a throwaway sentence about a variation commonly referred to as the Meliae. *The Meliae variation can bond with creatures that make their homes inside trees. This bond behaves similarly to the witches' bond with their familiar.* The author quickly moved on from that, but my eyes froze on the word *familiar.*

"That explains it."

"What?" Victor asked.

I read the sentence to him, my voice rising in triumph over the word familiar. "The bees. She must be a Meliae. She bonded with the bees."

"How do witches' familiars work?"

I stood and paced. "For witches, it makes them bigger, and they usually live longer. But more importantly, we become extremely close. I can feel Gertie. She can feel me. I know when she's feeling sad. And if something were to happen to me—if I died before she did—Gertie would mourn. I mean… the word *mourn* doesn't do it justice. It's a bone-deep sadness. It's despair so strong she might not survive it. For a familiar to lose the witch they've bonded with, it's… soul crushing. It's a grief so strong not even magic can touch it. Avery's bees must be grieving. And what do people do sometimes when they grieve? They get angry."

The corners of Victor's mouth quirked up.

"What?" I stared at him.

"Your familiar is a cow?"

I stiffened and straightened. I tilted my head back so I was looking at him down my nose. "They're not all cats. Gertie's been with me since I was a teenager, and she'll still be with me when I'm old and gray."

Victor grimaced. "I didn't mean anything bad by it. I mean, I guess I shouldn't be surprised. She was like your shadow the few times I went out to your farm. It's… I've always liked quirky things. It's refreshing."

I studied him a second longer. He didn't seem to be making fun of my familiar being a dairy cow. I had gotten used to people being judgmental about one of my best friends being a farm animal. It was hard not to feel protective of her.

I nodded and took my seat next to Victor. We skimmed over the last few sections. There were countless types of dryads, with other well-known varieties being the Leshy and Kodoma. The author griped some more about the inaccuracy of the name *dryad* before concluding with book recommendations for a more in-depth analysis.

"Was that helpful?" Victor asked.

"I think so." My eyes flicked over the entry again, searching for anything else of use. The biggest help was knowing why the bees were angry. I would probably need help from my coven to come up with ideas on how to deal with them. "I'm going to have to be careful about getting close to the hives. They are going to be grieving for a while."

"Good." Victor closed the book and leaned back in his chair. "What time was your first interview?"

I glanced at my phone. It was almost one o'clock, and I hadn't gotten much done. "I should probably head out."

Victor walked me to the door. "Until next time."

"Yeah." I hovered at the threshold. "I'm looking forward to learning more."

"Me too." He brushed a strand of my hair behind my ear. "Maybe next time, I can make something fancier than grilled cheese so we can take our time reading through the next entry together."

I nodded. My mouth was dry. *Is he flirting with me? He couldn't be, could he?* I jerked my thumb toward the door. "I'll, uh... get going to that interview."

I darted away and made my way to my truck, which was parked across the street. I didn't know how I was going to find Travis's pack to conduct my interview just yet, but I wasn't going to be able to figure it out on Victor's front porch. That man flustered me more than I wanted to admit. And somehow, he still wanted me to come back and continue reading the book with him.

He was just being nice. Stop reading into things.

CHAPTER 15

I drove a few blocks away and found a spot along the boardwalk. Parked there, I hunched over my phone in my truck, scrolling through Travis's social media. I squinted at the photos posted on his wall. Tracking magic wasn't my strong suit, so I was trying to figure out where I could find his pack the old-fashioned way. The same faces appeared over and over, and almost every one of the photos had been taken at a bar. After a few more minutes of poking around, I located the name of the bar—Wildwood Meadery. From there, it took me a few more minutes to find out that the meadery was owned and operated by Travis and Trinity Burrows. I didn't know much about werewolves, but based on the little pieces of folklore that I'd heard growing up, they tended to be family focused. If I was going to find his pack anywhere, it would be at that bar. I checked their hours. They didn't open until three, so I had time to kill before I tried to confirm his alibi.

I sat in my truck, debating with myself. I could switch up the order of my investigative tasks and try to find Diana or Russell, or I could head back to the farm for a few midday chores. Even with Lindsey's help, chores outside the standard maintenance were piling up. Though all the animals were fed and taken care of, I had some planting to do and a gutter in desperate need of repairs.

I opted for home. With gutter repairs on the brain, I jumped in my seat as the music from the radio shifted to the shrill ring of my phone. I jabbed the answer button on my steering wheel.

"This is Megan."

"Megan!" Betty's energetic voice flowed over the speakers.

"Of course it's Megan. That's who we called," Agnes cut in.

"We just arrived at the Grand Canyon. We would have called sooner," Sarah said.

"But we didn't have good signal until now," Betty finished.

They talk over each other for a few seconds, each exclaiming about how beautiful Arizona was and how difficult it was to drive an RV. The conversation was hard to follow but so quintessentially them that I couldn't help smiling. The three of them had always talked over each other yet still understood what the others were saying as if they had waited like a normal person for the other one to finish. I guess that was what happened when you grew up together and had been attached at the hip since diapers.

"Anyway…" Sarah's voice rose above the rest, drawing the group's attention to the matter at hand. "You had questions about Wardens and werewolves."

"Right." Betty cleared her throat. "Not that Point Pleasant isn't wonderful. It is. But now that we are on our little road trip, we've picked up a lot of things that we just didn't know."

"We've seen things. Heard things." Agnes's voice came out loud, like she was sitting too close to the mic. "It's wild. Apparently, the Wardens don't just police witches anymore. They police the supernatural community as a whole."

My jaw dropped as I tried to absorb what she'd just told me.

Sarah picked up where Agnes had left off. "Technically

speaking, there are now other types of supernaturals in their ranks. But it's still a majority-witch organization."

Betty sighed. "And as you can probably suspect, just like when they're dealing with witches, the Wardens assume guilt before innocence. Always."

I gripped the steering wheel, my eyes focused on the road ahead of me while my mind whirled. "So I take it they don't get along well with werewolves, then."

Agnes's tone became sad. "They don't get along well with anybody."

I groaned. "That's just great."

"Oh gosh. It looks like the tour group is gathering," Sarah said.

"We're going to be riding mules down into the canyon," Betty said.

Agnes giggled, either with delight or nerves—it was hard to tell. "Mules. Can you picture it?"

"We should get going before they leave without us," Sarah said.

"It was lovely talking to you, dear. Keep us updated!" Betty hung up before I could respond.

I stared blankly ahead as I continued driving home. The Wardens didn't get along well with anybody. That wasn't great news. But it definitely explained why Travis was so worked up when he found out I was working for them. If he was innocent—if he really thought I was assuming his guilt in front of his family—that would be hard.

But I wasn't like the Wardens. I knew what it was like to have people assume the worst, and I didn't want to do that to anyone. Not if I could help it.

Farm chores passed in a blur. Before I knew it, it was almost three o'clock, and I was dashing out the door to drive to the meadery. By then, traffic had picked up, and the trip took much longer than I would have liked. While it wasn't that far from Point Pleasant, by the time I'd made it past the various road-construction projects, it was almost five. I groaned and pulled into the parking lot, which was half filled with cars.

I stared at the building. With its sturdy logs and giant floor-to-ceiling windows, it looked more like a lodge than a bar. Above the front door was a sign, the words Wildwood Meadery painted in soft greens and outlined in gold. The place was both rustic and chic. I wasn't sure what I'd expected when I found out Travis owned a meadery, but it wasn't this. He seemed too rough around the edges. This place had a similar edge, but it was refined.

I grabbed Heather's green eye shadow and smeared it across my lids. I stared at my eyes in the rearview mirror and exhaled slowly. The red petals unique to my magic ghosted out of my mouth as I murmured the words to a simple illusion spell. The petals swirled around me and then sank into my skin. I watched as my green eyes became brown and my brown hair took on an even deeper hue. The illusion settled over me so completely it even changed the position of my freckles. After a few seconds, an entirely different woman was looking back at me. I had given myself a snowbird vibe. This was the time of year that they would be flocking back to the Pacific Northwest from somewhere warmer like Arizona. Satisfied with the illusion, I climbed out of the truck and sent off a quick text to my coven.

> At the Wildwood Meadery. Headed in to try and see if Travis really does have an alibi. Wish me luck.

> **Heather:**
> I've got my fingers crossed for you.

> **Kim:**
> Be careful.

Dani:
Update us after.

Heather:
I think I finally perfected the muffin recipe. Come by the café after closing and we can catch up while I experiment on you.

You say experiment, but all I hear is "come by the café and let me feed you delicious food."

Kim:
Same.

Heather:
I mean, true. But I felt I should be up front in case I've lost my mind after recipe twenty-seven and they are not actually that good.

Dani:
Your cooking is always good.

I'll be there.

I tucked my phone into my pocket. Halfway across the parking lot, I faltered. I was doing my usual stride, which included a slight stomp. It helped put people off so they didn't try to talk to me. This was a mission to confirm an alibi. I had to make myself approachable. Closing my eyes, I pictured the friendliest person I knew—Heather. I tried to recall how she walked and emulated it as best I could as I made my way into the meadery. As the doors swung shut behind me, I gulped. My gaze bounced from patron to patron, my heartbeat racing as I lost count of how many supernaturals were inside. They each had a similar vibrant, almost mossy-green light hulking a few feet over their heads in an almost wolfish shape. I had found Travis's pack, and there were a lot of them.

I forced my legs to continue moving and strolled casually

toward the bar. Heather always had a slight bounce to her step that gave off a carefree vibe, so I tried to channel that. I came to a stop by the bar and slid onto a stool near one of the few guys who was alone. He had the same glow as the rest of the room.

He turned to me, a flirtatious smile on his lips. "I don't think I've seen you in here before."

"First time. I'm just settling in for the summer. Is it always this full?"

"Yeah." He leaned against the bar and held his bear bottle up to his lips. "It belongs to a good friend of mine. We spend most nights here."

"Most nights? Even Fridays?" I tried to add a teasing tone to my voice. By the hooded look his eyes took on, I might have hit the mark too well.

"Especially Fridays." He leaned toward me. "Fridays are the best day here. We can really let loose."

"Really?" I shifted to face him. "Maybe I should come by on a Friday, then."

He inhaled deeply. His brow furrowed as he studied me, and a look of disappointment flashed in his eyes. "This place has great dinners. But after that, Travis usually shuts the doors so it's just friends and family. You know, making sure it's people we have things in common with."

I raised an eyebrow. "Every Friday? Wouldn't he lose out on a ton of money that way?"

"Nah. Family can spend just as much money as nonfamily. Last Friday, this place was packed for Shorty's birthday. He was turning twenty-one. Well, technically on Saturday. We had a massive party. Travis must have grilled a hundred steaks, and then at midnight, we rang it in with shots and the biggest cake I've ever seen. Trinity really outdid herself on that one."

"That sounds like a great time." I smiled. "Although I've seen some impressive cakes. I doubt it was really that big."

He barked out a laugh and fished his phone out of his pocket. He scrolled through a few photos and then turned the screen toward me. It was a group shot of a bunch of guys with smiles and shot glasses standing around a cake that was easily six tiers tall and several feet wide. Shorty, who looked like he might have been a linebacker, towered over the cake, with a grin plastered across his face. My eyes bounced around the photo until I located Travis in the background, plating a huge stack of steaks. If this picture was taken at midnight, there was no way Travis could have been out at Avery's property that night and gotten back here in time to flip steaks.

"Hey, Chad?" someone yelled from across the bar.

The guy I was with gave me an apologetic smile and sauntered off to talk to whoever had called him. I turned to the bar, scanning the bottles behind it. There was a full bar on one side and, on the other, row upon row of mead bottles with the Wildwood Meadery logo stamped across them. I quickly ordered myself a bottle to go and was headed for the door with my purchase wrapped up in a paper bag when Travis stepped out in front of me.

I stumbled to a stop. "Excuse me," I mumbled as I side-stepped him.

Travis moved backward to cut me off and glowered. "You may look different, but you don't smell different. What are you doing in at my bar?"

My skin prickled as I noted the change in the room. No one was speaking. Everyone had averted their gaze, but I could tell I had the attention of everyone there. I swallowed and gripped the bottle tight. "The same thing I was doing at your house—investigating a murder."

He snorted. "Typical. Someone dies, and a witch suspects a wolf."

My gaze flicked to Chad. He looked confused. I didn't think he'd been playing me during our conversation. He'd told me about the birthday party before anyone knew I was here. My gut told me Travis had a rock-solid alibi. He was just too used to witches looking at him like he was lesser than them.

I looked him in the eye. "You have an alibi. You're not a suspect anymore."

He blinked and shifted closer. He sniffed at me. "Say that again."

"You're not a suspect."

He cocked his head and inhaled one more time. "You're not lying."

"You can smell when people are lying?" I asked.

He shrugged. "It's an alpha thing."

"Well, then take a deep breath. I *really* am just looking for the killer. I may be a liaison for the Wardens, but I'm not one of them. I'm a Point Pleasant resident first."

He inhaled deeply, nodded, then stepped back. "Enjoy the mead."

I slipped past him and marched to my truck. I held it together until I was behind the steering wheel, but once my truck door closed, my whole body shook. I had just been surrounded by werewolves, and the only thing that got me out of it was the fact that I was telling the truth.

I silently cursed Miranda. The liaison position had even more baggage than I'd anticipated. At least my next interviewee, Diana, wouldn't know about the connection, assuming she wasn't secretly paranormal as well. I just had to ask an older woman about her potential eviction.

CHAPTER 16

The sun was dipping low on the horizon as I approached Diana's place, riding on the back of Gertie. She was snorting to make sure I was aware of how annoyed she felt that we were once again trekking around in the woods after dark. I could feel her incredulity through our bond. She didn't understand how there were two houses without road access that I needed to go to multiple times. I patted her between the shoulders as we came to a stop at the white picket fence around Diana's place. The lights were out, leaving the windows dark.

I swung down from the saddle and made my way to the front door. It didn't look any more inviting close up than it did from a distance. My knuckles hovered over the door. *Maybe she's asleep.* It wasn't even eight o'clock yet. While a bit late for a house call, the hour wasn't unreasonable.

I knocked. Silence greeted me. I strained my ears for any sign of someone moving around inside. Nothing. I knocked again and held my breath, waiting. No one came to the door. I stepped back and walked around the home. Every light was out. Either Diana had gone to bed, or she was out.

I backtracked to Gertie and climbed back on. "Sorry, girl. It looks like it was a wasted trip."

Gertie let out a dramatic sigh.

I glanced up at the sky and found the moon. I studied its shape and position and readjusted myself on the saddle. "If we go that way, we can cut right through the forest on our way back into town. Plus, I'm sure Heather will let you snag a few of her muffins."

Gertie picked up speed, going from a slow meander to a canter. I grinned as we barreled through the trees. Gertie was a sucker for Heather's cooking. Whenever Heather came to visit, she spoiled Gertie rotten.

After a few minutes Gertie slowed to trot so she wouldn't tire herself out. I loosened my hold on her reins and leaned back in my seat. Icy wind wrapped around me, cooling my heated skin. There was something exhilarating about riding. I tipped my head back, breathing in and smiling up at the trees.

A light moved off to the right. I jerked my head toward it and slowed Gertie with my knees. I peered into the darkness. The light continued to move. It was going away from me at an angle. I turned Gertie toward it, and we crept forward until I could make out what it was—a lantern moving in the night.

"What on earth?" I murmured.

It wasn't moving fast. Someone was walking through the trees by lantern light. Gertie ambled closer and came to a stop when we hit the edge of Avery's meadow. The lantern was moving around past the white picket fence.

I slid off Gertie's back and patted her side. "Stay here, girl."

Gertie rubbed her head against my cheek. I gave her a quick hug then stepped away to sneak along the tree line. I tracked the direction the lantern was moving and skirted along the tree line to intercept. As I got closer, the figure holding the lantern took shape. They were petite, with light hair. They came to a stop a few feet from the beehives. I inched closer until I could make out who it was. Diana.

I crouched and slunk past the tree line and under the fence. I padded forward. A soft voice drifted to me from her position. It was lifted in song. I couldn't make heads or tails of the words. They weren't English. They had a lilting quality and almost sounded like a hymn. I studied Diana in the dim light. From where I hid, she didn't look any different from when I'd met her at her cabin. She looked like she didn't possess a supernatural aura.

I took another step closer to make sure, and a twig snapped under me. I froze. Her song continued but was joined by buzzing. I shuffled back as the buzzing grew louder. I wouldn't be able to get closer without the bees coming out, and without my coven to lend a hand, I wouldn't be able to get out without at least a few more stings. The worst of the swelling from the previous beestings had gone down, but they still ached on occasion when my shirt rubbed against them.

I retreated to the fence and scurried back to Gertie before Diana came back that way. I didn't know what she was doing near the hive, but if it was something that would make the bees more aggressive, I wanted to make sure I was prepared before I had that confrontation.

As the Bizzy Bean came into view, I relaxed, swaying in the saddle. Gertie lumbered the last few steps to the parking spots near the front door. I hopped down and put down a few reflective cones from a saddle bag, so people could clearly see Gertie standing there, then headed into the café to meet up with my coven. When I entered, the rest of them were already at our usual booth in the back. I locked up behind me and pushed open the doors to the plexiglass cat enclosure. Charlie, Dani's familiar, scampered around the room, letting his mother, Star, chase him. He was massive, well over thirty pounds, and his much smaller mother had no way of catching up to him without him modulating his pace. He slowed at the turn at the end of the room so she could pounce.

I grinned down at them as I crossed the room to claim the last spot at the booth. "I promised Gertie a few muffins, so I hope you have some to spare."

Heather pushed a box across the table to me. "For her, always."

I peered inside. There was an extra-large muffin just for Gertie. "Thank you."

"Don't thank me yet. You haven't tried them. I can't believe I let Becca talk me into adding morning glory muffins to the menu. They've been a beast to get right." Heather slid a plate to the center of the table.

We all reached out to grab one. I bit into mine. It was delicious.

"Amazing as always," Kim said.

Heather sagged into her seat. "Thank god. If I had to try another variation, I was going to lose my mind. But now that the taste testing is done, let's move on to more important matters. Spill. How'd the alibi verification go?"

"Better than I expected." I quickly filled them in on how my day had gone, ending with the unusual Diana sighting at the apiary. "That leaves the only suspects as Diana and Russell. I'm leaning more toward Diana, given the strange behavior in the woods, and Russell just... doesn't entirely feel right, you know? His fear of the bee he saw was legit. I have a hard time picturing him standing next to her hives and hitting her over the head with a rifle. I also can't help but feel I need to get a closer look at those hives, which might be difficult if the bees are in mourning."

"We could try a shield amulet to keep the bees away," Kim said.

I smiled. "That sounds like a great idea."

"I'll grab the supplies." Heather slipped out of the booth and headed to her supply closet. She always made sure we had what we needed to cast when we were here.

Dani tapped her fingers on the table. "That should help with the bees. Is there anything else you need help with?"

My inadequacies flitted through my mind. I opened my mouth to say I was good when Kim looked over.

She pointed at me. "Don't you dare say 'nothing.'"

I grimaced. "I should be able to figure it out on my own."

Dani squeezed my hand. "We're a coven. We're supposed to have each other's backs, or did you learn nothing when we were facing off against Meredith Walker?"

I'm supposed to have your back. I forced the negative self-talk to the back of my mind. Dani was right. I had to face it. "I suck at divination magic. I don't know the first thing about using it."

Dani smiled. "Remind me to show you my gran's journal on the sight. It was super helpful. In the meantime, let's work on my favorite trick—reading emotions from an object."

While Kim prepared the ingredients and Heather dashed off to the kitchen for much-needed hot chocolate, Dani walked me through what she claimed were the simple steps involved in reading objects. By the time she was done, I had successfully identified one correct emotion. It took more energy than most other spells, and she could do it like it was nothing. I still wasn't sure how I was supposed to fill her shoes while investigating.

"You ready to make the amulet?" Kim asked.

I sipped hot chocolate to restore my reserves and nodded. "Let's do it."

Casting with my coven came naturally to me at this point. We handed our magic back and forth. Kim was a whiz at protection magic, so Dani and I funneled our magic into her while she worked. Her hands were graceful as she tied the magic to the black tourmaline. It was beautiful to watch.

Kim handed the tourmaline off to me. "Just utter the activation word, and it'll kick in. The spell should hold for at least a week, which should be plenty of time."

We chatted for a few more minutes and split up for the night. I carried Gertie's muffin out to her, and then we ambled home in the cooling air of late spring. Now that I had an amulet to protect me from the bees, I felt a lot more confident about my looming face-off with Diana.

CHAPTER 17

The next morning, I rode Gertie back out to Diana's place. I dismounted and then glanced back at Gertie. She was supposed to wait patiently by the fence, but she'd edged around it and was standing halfway through the gate, her big brown eyes staring at me in concern. I waved her back and held up the protection amulet. She took one shuffled step backward but refused to exit the yard completely.

I smiled at her and turned back to the door I stood in front of. The night before, I'd boldly knocked on it, but in the morning light, I hesitated. Watching Diana calmly sing to bees that wanted to sting me to death had been unnerving. *How am I supposed to look her in the face?* I clenched my fists, squared my shoulders, and rapped my knuckles against the wood.

The door swung inward, and Diana peered out at me through blurry eyes. Her graying hair was mussed, and she was wrapped up in a fluffy blue robe. The hem was tattered, and there was paint splattered on the sleeves.

"I had a few more questions for you," I said.

She blinked at me and took a step back. "I was just about to make tea. Do you want some?"

I followed her inside. "That would be lovely."

Diana offered me a seat and shuffled into the kitchen to take the kettle off the stove. "Is peppermint okay? I've been trying to cut down on caffeine. It makes me jittery."

I nodded and sat. As she moved around the kitchen, I noticed that the dark forest painting she had been working on previously looked like it was almost done. She'd added an amazing amount of detail, including a beam of light coming down that highlighted a single white flower in the middle of the darkened trees. It was beautiful.

Diana flopped down across from me and rubbed at her eyes. "What do you need to know?"

I placed my hand, palm down, on the table and watched where she placed her hands to make sure she touched it too. I mentally went through the directions Dani had given me the previous night. It still blew my mind that this came naturally to her and I had to funnel a ton of magical energy to make it work. I exhaled. The translucent rose petals that were a manifestation of my magic flowed out of my mouth, trailed down my arm, and sank into the skin of my hand. A hollowness formed in my chest, and my heartbeat slowed. My whole body felt heavy. I tried cataloguing the sensation to figure out what emotion it was. Dani always just knew, but it took me a second to land on the answer—depressed.

"I found the eviction paperwork."

She flinched, my words hanging in the air between us. A single tear streaked down her cheek, and she wiped it away. I exhaled another cloud of magical energy and continued to focus on the sensations I picked up through the table. My heart ached, and a heaviness spread through my body. There was no denying the effect my words had on her. They broke her heart.

Her voice wavered as she spoke. "I really thought I would be able to talk Avery out of it. When she told me she wanted me out of here, I didn't believe her. I didn't think she would do it. Maybe she wouldn't have. She never officially filed the paperwork, but she did wave them in my face when I saw her last. We were friends for years. How could she just want me gone after all this time, after... after she was there for me when my husband died? It didn't make any sense."

"You sound like you still care about her."

"I do." She shook her head, a choked laugh coming out of her. It was wet with sadness. "I can't just shut off ten years of friendship. I was going to fix it. I just hadn't figured out how yet."

"I saw you last night," I said.

She stiffened. "What?"

"You were singing to the bees." I exhaled another gust of power into my hands.

My stomach tightened in hunger. I would need to eat again soon if I kept this up. Through the table, I could feel Diana's stomach dropping and her becoming lightheaded as a flush crept up the sides of her neck.

She cringed. "Ever since she died, her bees have been worked up. I figured they were grieving. She always said they were smarter than we gave them credit for."

"But why sing?"

She shrugged. "I used to watch Avery do it. She sang to them while she worked. I must have listened to her sing that same old song a thousand times. I thought... I thought if I could sing it like she did, they wouldn't feel so lonely. It didn't work, though. I'm not as good a singer."

My hand shook against the table as I kept up the contact and the flow of magic. Everything—her words and the way she acted—lined up with the feelings I was receiving through the table. I had to be sure, though.

"Can you tell me about the last time you saw her?"

"Is this really helpful?" she asked.

My shoulders tensed. Fighting my normal urge to hide

how I was feeling, I let my face soften. "I want to find who hurt your friend."

"Okay." She shuddered. "It was a few days after she told me she wanted me gone. I had given her some space. I kept hoping I would bump into her at one of our usual spots, but she had become such a recluse. So I baked and went over to her house with a plate of cookies to try and reconnect. She wouldn't let me in. We had our last conversation standing on her front doorstep. She kept saying she knew what I was trying to do. That I was just like her neighbor who was trying to steal her land. That I wouldn't get away with it. She waved the eviction paperwork in my face and yelled about how I was greedy. She said some vile things and slammed the door in my face. I wish I knew what she was talking about. But she was so sure her neighbor was trying to steal from her, and that I was in cahoots with him somehow, that she wouldn't let me get a word in. I've never seen her so angry."

Her despair rolling into me from my connection to the table became overwhelming. I gasped and yanked my hand back. Diana was crying into her hands, her elbows resting on the table. I had just put this poor woman through the wringer. Her shoulders shook as she sobbed.

"I miss my friend. But that day? It was like she was already gone. I would give anything to get her back."

I patted her shoulder as she cried. I didn't know what to do. The only person left on my list was Russell, and I hadn't found a single piece of evidence, outside of rumors, linking him to Avery. It wasn't enough.

I'm messing this up. The council shouldn't have trusted me with this. I've got nothing, and they're counting on me to figure out who did it so the right agency can make the arrest. Even Miranda would have done better, assuming she didn't stop at Travis.

Diana's crying stopped after a few minutes. She wiped at her eyes and shuffled back to the kitchen with her full mug of tea. "The water's cold now. I'll need to make another."

"Thank you for your time."

I hovered by the kitchen table before turning and leaving through the front door. If she was anything like me, she wouldn't appreciate someone gawking at her when she was feeling so raw. I retreated to Gertie and climbed up onto her back. I sagged into my saddle. There had to be something I was missing—something more concrete that would tie Russell to Avery's death.

I turned Gertie toward Avery's house. Now that I had my protection amulet on, I could get closer to the hives. If I could find something there, it would make my next conversation with Russell a lot more productive. As I rode away from Diana's, I did my best to quiet the voice that told me I was a failure. If only my feigned confidence could fool myself.

CHAPTER 18

I left Gertie at the gate and trudged toward the hives. My internal critic had only grown louder as I rode over to the apiary. The word *failure* repeated in my mind. I wasn't done yet, but the thought of standing before city council again, with what little I had to show, made my heart stutter. The only thing pointing to Russell was a rumor of a border dispute. But I hadn't found a single piece of physical evidence linking him to it. I needed more. I needed something that would trigger a confession or something. If all I had to report when I spoke to the councilors next was an unconfirmed rumor, they would rethink their decision to select me for the liaison position. Maybe that wouldn't be so bad. I would get my time back. But then for the rest of my life, every time I came into town, people would know how much of a failure I was. I was just getting used to people liking me. I didn't want to go from the town pariah to the town joke. Plus, if I messed this up, it could leave people like Travis relying on Miranda not to jump to conclusions.

The buzzing of the hives cut through my thoughts. I steeled myself and muttered the word that would activate the protection spell. It should last at least twenty minutes before

I needed to activate it again. I marched forward, ignoring the growing noise, and crouched down in front of the hives. I flinched when the first bee hit the protective shield around me. They rained down on it like hail.

I willed myself to continue onward. *They can't hurt you. Not right now. Get in. Get out. Find evidence.*

I grabbed hold of the wooden carving hanging from twine under the hive and pulled it out into the light. The wood had been anointed over and over again with myrrh oil, which had mixed with honey that had dripped down onto it from the hives, giving it a rough-around-the-edges look. Under the layers of oil, grime, and sticky honey, it was exactly like the ones Jessica had in her shop. It was a witch's knot, for protection. I relaxed my eyes as if I were looking at a piece of art containing a hidden image and checked it for magical residue. There wasn't anything left on it. I dropped it, and it swung under the hive, bouncing around at the end of the string.

I stood and walked around the hives in a slowly expanding circle. The bees continued to buzz around me, crowding the edges of my protective shield. I squinted between them at the ground as my path took me between the flowers. There was nothing unusual there. New growth poked out. I shifted my fingers through the loose soil where it had recently been dug up to plant more bulbs. Avery used a soil mix of peat moss, compost, and vermiculite. It was a bit grayer than normal, and it shimmered as it flowed through my fingertips. I dropped my hands to my sides and continued my spiral one small step at a time.

In front of me, a small patch of earth was more disturbed than the others. I knelt down next to it and pushed some of the leaves aside. Pressed perfectly into the soil was a boot print. It was only two feet away from where the evidence cones were clustered, and it looked almost identical to the mold I had put together farther into the woods—except this one was of the other shoe. I smiled and fumbled around in my pocket for a Payday bar. There were probably healthier snacks, but I was a sucker for peanuts with caramel. I munched on it to make sure I would have the energy for a spell to create another mold. I had neglected to eat that day. All magic required energy, and casting too much could do terrible things to my blood sugar.

As I swallowed the last of the candy, I snapped a few photos of the footprint then clenched and unclenched my hands to settle my nerves. I ignored the bees as they continued to swarm around me and murmured the words to the spell that would pluck some soil from a few feet away and turn it into a mold of the footprint. The dirt flashed red and then settled into my hands—leaving me with a perfect mold of the second footprint.

I continued my perusal, but nothing stood out. *What am I missing?* I stood stock-still at the edge of the fence, my eyes darting between the house and the hives as the protection shield dissipated around me. I was far enough back that the bees didn't care about me anymore. But no matter where I looked, I found nothing. There were no new clues other than the footprint. I would need to come up with some sort of justification to ask to see a second pair of Russell's boots, since the first pair were not a match.

My gaze slid over the tree line as I turned back to Gertie. I froze. Something was out of place. I turned my head, studying the trees and the ground. It was like one of those puzzles they put in kids' magazines when I was growing up, which had you highlight all the ways one image was not like the other. It was always small things, like the clock reading a different time or eyes pointing in a different direction. Except I didn't have the first image to compare it to. I only had the memory of walking this way, and I'd only done it once in daylight. I'd always been good at that game, and I could feel that something had changed.

I stalked forward, my eyes darting from one tree to another. When I'd left Avery's cottage the first day, I'd been in a rush. The bees were aggressive, and someone was outside. John Barfield. I made my way to where his ATV had been. He'd parked between a large gray oak and a pile of rocks painted white to mark the boundary. I faltered as I located the tree. The rocks were no longer perpendicular to it and the fence. They were five feet forward.

I cocked my head, staring at them. *But Russell lives on the other side. Why would he move these stones?*

That thought made me wonder if I was remembering their position correctly. There was no reason Russell would move stones on this side of the property. Unless he wasn't the neighbor Avery had a border dispute with. *Didn't someone mention him by name?* I wished I had a better memory for conversations. Remembering visuals was easy, but the words someone said were much harder, maybe because so much of my life had been lived in silence. But knowing where I'd left things, so I could identify when someone had snuck onto my property for another prank—that had been useful.

Gertie shuffled up next to me and rested her head against my shoulder. I patted her on the side of her large skull, my fingers finding their way up to scratch behind her ears. She snuffled at my shoulder.

"I'm just trying to figure it out," I murmured. "Were the stones farther back last time?"

She sighed dramatically and bobbed her head in an exaggerated shrug. While my neighbors' kids used to paint her blue on occasion, none of their pranks ever got to her. She didn't care what color she was so long as she got snacks out of the deal. I continued to scratch her ears as I thought over the problem.

Gertie jerked her head up and to the side. She did it two more times. I followed her line of sight to a crow perched on the branches of a nearby tree. While she might not know if someone had moved the stones, she might have just alerted me to a witness.

I released my grip on Gertie and inched toward the bird. I blew a cloud of translucent red petals at him, imbuing them with a calming but inviting feeling. I needed to convince the crow to come close enough for me to touch him. The bird cocked his head and hopped along the branch in my direction. He jumped from one tree limb to another and then stopped a few feet overhead. I raised my arm, held it parallel to the ground, and blew out another swirl of inviting magic toward him. His wings flared out to the sides, and he swooped down to land on my arm. Tentatively, I reached up and stroked his cheek.

"Well, aren't you a beautiful boy," I whispered.

He nuzzled my hand, his eyes closing. With my fingers, I rubbed the top of his head, between his eyes, and to the edge of his beak.

With him comfortable on my arm, I murmured the words to the first spell I'd ever learned. It didn't exactly let me speak with animals, but it forged a connection between me and an animal I was touching. I could ask questions and get an impression of his memories. They were always a bit disjointed. Different animals focused on different things. But because I'd spent most of my life on a farm, surrounded by wildlife, animals had sometimes been my only friends, and this was the only way I knew how to communicate on a deeper level.

The bird blinked at me as the connection snapped into place. It wasn't as strong as a familiar bond, but I could feel his curiosity thrumming in my chest as he stared at my face. If the spell could have worked on something as simplistic as a bee, I would have tried it at the hive.

The crow cawed in greeting—a friendly hello.

"Do you live around here?"

I got flashes of images. They were all of this forest, the

edge of town, and the apiary. One tree repeated over and over. It was the gray oak. He liked to nest in the crotch because it was high up and he could see all over while still feeling safe with the massive branches spreading out around him.

"Good." I turned us so the white stones were in his line of sight. "Those white stones—did they used to be someplace else?"

Images of him returning to the tree, day in and day out, flashed in my mind. The seasons changed. The stones were always in the same spot—perpendicular to the tree. They had moved.

"Did you see who moved the stones?"

The image in my mind was dark. The crow was in his nest. He peered down at a man whose back was turned. It was hard to make any details out. Crows did not have the best night vision, and this must have been twilight. It was definitely a man, and one who drove an angry-sounding beast, which I recognized as an ATV. After the stones were moved, the beast had prowled away from the crow's nest, going in the opposite direction of Russell's property. Whoever had moved the stones wasn't Russell. It was another neighbor. And the only other neighbor I knew about who lived out this way was John Barfield, the guy running against Amanda Yu for city council.

CHAPTER 19

It didn't take me long to find the ATV tracks. I walked Gertie along them. In most places, they were easy enough to follow, but in sections where the game trail opened up, they were harder to find without being closer to the ground than I could get from Gertie's back. The trail ended at another property line. That one had a barbed wire fence and a padlocked gate. I crouched down next to the lock and examined it. I ran my fingers over the worn edges. It was a standard lock that I could buy in bulk at the hardware store, a fact I knew because over the years, one of the pranks that kids would pull on my property would be to put random locks on things. I didn't have any of my tools with me, but that didn't matter. I had other ways to open the locks.

I lowered myself farther and yanked up the padlock as far as it would go so I could peer into the keyhole. While the tumblers weren't visible, I could direct the magic if I could at least see the hole I was pushing it through. With my eyes focused on the lock, I murmured the words to a spell that gave me very limited telekinetic abilities. I sent the tendril of power forward. Sweat sprang up across my brow as I contracted the power till it was as narrow as a lockpick and guided it into the lock. I closed my eyes and focused on what I could sense, doing my best to ignore the strain on my knee or the uncomfortable way my jeans dug into my stomach. A small smile crossed my lips as I found the tumblers. After a few seconds of fumbling about inside the lock, I found the correct positions and pressed down. The lock popped open in my hand.

I set the lock aside and opened the gate. Gertie shuffled closer and hit my shoulder with her head. Her concern flowed into me through our bond. I scratched at the side of her head again as I pulled out my phone. "I feel you. I know you're worried. Would it make you feel better if I texted the others to let them know where I am?"

Gertie sagged against me, resting a small amount of weight on my side. I stiffened, and I stumbled to the left. She was much too big to lean on me anymore. Chuckling, I typed out a message to my coven.

> It looks like the neighbor Avery was having a boundary dispute with was John Barfield.
>
> I'm at his property now. Going to try and interview him.

I put my phone away, walked through the gate, and strode across the yard to John's home. He lived in a two-story farmhouse painted a bright yellow that shone in the midday sun. I stared straight at the front door as I took in my surroundings through my peripheral vision. I marched toward the door. The porch creaked under me as I climbed the steps. Closer to the house, it looked like it had been recently painted but over old, cracked siding. That was like putting lipstick on a pig. Underneath, the house was still worn down.

I rapped against the front door with my knuckles. There were no roads nearby. In the relative quiet of the property, the knock was loud. I hovered at the front door, waiting. I held my breath, my ears straining to hear movement inside.

After almost half a minute I exhaled sharply. No one had moved inside the house. I took a step back, and the porch groaned under me as I studied the front of the house. Bright-white curtains hung in the windows, hiding whatever lay beyond.

I knocked one more time and listened. When no one responded, I turned on my heel and made my way around the side of the house. While the man of the house might not have been home, I could still get a feel for him by looking around. My gaze slid from window to window. Each one was filled with that same type of white curtain. There was something impersonal about it. The paint and curtains were like a veneer over the home, designed to give the impression of someone doing well. But if the curtains were anything like the paint, I was sure that hidden behind them was a home in disrepair.

I stopped at the rear of the house when the back door came into view. From there, I could see into the house. The back door was open, with only a simple storm door between me and the rest of the house. I glanced around. There was no one in sight. I inched forward and peered into the house. Beyond the storm door was a mudroom with an old washer and dryer and a large industrial-style sink. The linoleum on the floors was chipped and curled at the corners.

And piled in the middle of the room were campaign signs attached to stakes, dirt clinging to the wood. I stood up on tiptoes to get a better view. Amanda's face, with her black hair and slate-gray eyes, stared out at me, her white teeth flashing in a professional smile. I pressed against the storm door, craning my neck. My breath caught in my throat when my gaze landed on a pair of muddy boots. *Could they be...?*

I stepped back and looked around again. There was still no one in the yard. I knocked on the back door, my fist a bit more urgent than on my first two rounds of knocking. No one came to the door. Nothing stirred inside the house. I swayed in indecision. I reached out to test the storm door. If it was locked, I would come back later with backup.

It wasn't. The storm door swung open under my hand. I froze in the doorway then scurried inside and crouched down next to the boots. I flipped my backpack around and pulled out the molds I had made. My fingers squeezed the hard, reddened earth as I picked up the boots and compared them to the molds. The treads were a perfect match.

My breath came out ragged as I carefully propped the boots and the molds against the signs so everything was lined up. I snapped a photo and was leaning forward to grab the molds when tires crunched against gravel outside. I surged to my feet and darted toward the back door, then I stumbled to a stop when the passenger-side fender of a white truck came into view. The truck door slammed. I peered around the corner of the door as John emerged from his truck, a rifle in his hand.

My mouth went dry, and I scrambled backward from the door. My mind whirled. I had no justification for being in his house. *And if he did kill Avery, what is stopping him from killing me?* Before he reached the back porch, I spun on my heel and dashed into the next room. I darted through the house, taking in the threadbare carpet and peeling paint. I threw open the door to a closet under the stairs, clambered inside, and closed the door as quietly as I could.

My fingers shook as I fumbled with my phone in the dark. I pulled up Chris's number and dropped a pin with my current location.

I think I found the killer.

"Megan Miller?" John's voice came out almost in a singsong. "I know you're here."

CHAPTER 20

My heart leapt into my throat. I clamped a hand over my mouth to keep myself quiet. Footsteps echoed in the house on the other side of the door. I inched backward, curling inward as I squished myself into a corner behind a box I could barely make out in the darkness.

John's heavy footfalls grew louder. "I saw your cow outside. So thoughtful of you to leave her on the other side of the fence. I've never been a fan of fresh manure."

I stared at the door, willing it to stay closed. My palms were sweaty. I held one over my mouth and pressed the other into my stomach. My fingers shook against me.

"I'm not sure what you think you've found. While trespassing, I might add. But I'm sure we can talk about it. I'm a reasonable man."

My phone lit up with an incoming call. Fortunately, I had it on silent. I thumbed the volume-down button on the side as I answered it. I could barely hear him say my name through the speaker. I shoved it in my pocket, with the microphone pointed up so Chris could hear what was going on.

"Just come out. We can talk about this. Like adults."

I pressed my back against the back wall as he prowled closer. I blinked against the bright light as the door was flung open. John towered over me in the doorway, the rifle still in his hands.

He scowled at me. "Found you. Now, tell me. What have you found? What are you doing in my house uninvited?"

Panic surged through me. Everything about how he stood screamed danger. His finger was on the trigger. He loomed, his feet planted wide and his body angled over me. His eyes were wide, showing their whites, and a vein throbbed in his forehead. His neck muscles flexed as his nostrils flared.

I narrowed my eyes at him. If he was going to hurt me, then I would make sure Chris knew exactly why. I reached inside myself for my magic and grabbed the part of it that I despised—which I'd locked away and ignored for so long it was atrophied from disuse—and I pulled it out. It was the part of me that could make people do anything, the part I'd inherited from my mother. She'd used it against my father to strip him of his free will and make him stay. It was so weak that I could only force John to do one thing—talk.

"Tell me what you think I found." I unleashed the magic inside me.

A red swirl of magic engulfed him and sank into his skin. His body went rigid as his mouth opened of its own accord. "Proof that I killed Avery. As if she didn't deserve to die. Always acting like she was better than me. Lording the land my dad sold to her over my head. It was mine. I deserved it back! And then she had the audacity to back Amanda after promising to help me. I'm the real victim here."

I sagged as the last of my magic left me. My legs shook, and I struggled to stay upright. It had been so long since I'd accessed that part of me that even a simple use of it had exhausted me.

"I shouldn't have said that." He scowled and raised the rifle.

Time seemed to slow as he pointed it at my face. I screamed the activation word for the protective shield Kim had painstakingly made for me. She'd only meant it to stop bees, not bullets. I stared wide-eyed at his finger as he pulled the trigger. My ears rang as a loud pop filled the tiny space. A fraction of a second later, pain seared through my chest. All the air from my lungs was pushed out. A rib cracked. I felt like I'd been kicked by a horse. The tourmaline stone around my neck cracked and fell to the ground.

John's brow furrowed, his eyes narrowing in on my chest. I looked down. There was no blood or hole in the shirt. The bullet lay on the ground between my knees, broken, like it had hit something hard. My head snapped up as he readjusted the rifle.

I shoved my hand toward him and willed magic to the surface. My vision blurred, and my arm trembled as an alarmingly small number of red petals gusted toward him. "Sleep."

John swayed on his feet, the rifle slipping out of his grasp. He collapsed to the floor. The impacted jolted him, and his eyes opened back up. He pushed against the ground, his head swinging from side to side as he tried to clear it. Adrenaline coursed through me. I surged to my feet and darted past him down the hall. I threw myself at the front door, wrenched it open, and stumbled out onto the porch.

The bright light of the sun blinded me for a moment. I squinted out at the yard. Behind me, floorboards creaked. Footsteps shuffled after me. I couldn't wait for my eyes to adjust. I flung myself forward and tripped down the front steps onto my hands and knees.

The house continued to creak behind me. I scrambled forward, lurched to a standing position, and dashed away from the house, making a beeline for the closest cluster of trees.

"You can't outrun a bullet!" John yelled behind me.

I didn't look back. Instead, I ducked down to make myself a smaller target and continued forward with all my might. My legs burned. My vision swam, the trees appearing to double. Every inch of my body trembled as I pushed myself past the breaking point. I rushed into the tree line as another loud pop rang out behind me. Wood splintered a few inches from my head. I tumbled then crawled around the closest tree. With another popping sound, more bark exploded. My legs were so tired I couldn't even properly pull them up. I sat there, leaning against the tree, and hoped his gun would jam or that he would run out of bullets before he got to me.

My head jerked toward a loud crashing sound to my right. Gertie charged through the chain-link fence and dragged the strips of metal and posts behind her as she barreled toward the house. I couldn't get my arms or legs to cooperate. I could only watch as she stampeded across the yard. I cried out as John turned his rifle on her, but he didn't get it up in time. She rammed her head against his hand, sending the gun spiraling away. Then she pressed forward, shoving her weight against him and pinning him to the side of the house.

Leaning against the tree, I kept my eyes open through sheer force of will. I had used too much magic and run too far. All I wanted to do was sleep. Or eat. But instead, I stared into John's eyes as Gertie held him captive. As John struggled against her, sirens blared in the distance. She weighed over two thousand pounds. She didn't move unless she wanted to. And at the moment, all her rage was funneled into making sure he didn't get away.

My head lolled back as Chris's cruiser sped up to the house. I watched Gertie and John's feet as Chris and Harrison ran across the yard.

Chris kneeled down next to me and looked me over. "Were you hit?"

"Too much magic," I murmured. My eyelids were so heavy.

Harrison's voice carried to me from the house. "Jonathan Barfield, you are under arrest for the murder of Avery McGlynn and the attempted murder of Megan Miller. Anything you say can and will be used against you in a court of law."

Chris picked me up from the ground. The last thing I saw before the world went dark was Harrison slapping a set of handcuffs on John.

CHAPTER 21

My head pounded from the roller coaster that had happened the day before. John was arrested. Chris whisked me off to the emergency room because of my low blood sugar. They had me pumped full of glucose within minutes of my arrival, then I spent the next few hours trying to convince the doctors I wasn't diabetic.

Sleep had come late and the morning too early. The farm chores had to get done. I only had a few minutes to shower and get dressed before I was out the door again. I did my best to make myself look refreshed, throwing on a bit of makeup, including a bit of the green eye shadow Heather had gifted me. When I'd first put it on, I thought the color was a bit too bright for me, but it had grown on me, and I liked how it made my eyes pop. The added benefit of being able to see who was supernatural was a nice perk.

I shuffled into the city council chambers. It was half full, with over twenty people sitting in the audience. On one side of the room sat the councilors in their usual positions. They were all dressed almost exactly the same as the last time, except that Helen wore a black cardigan. While none of the city council members had a supernatural aura, almost everyone in the crowded audience glowed. My gaze bounced around, taking it all in. Seated at a table right in front of the banister that separated the city council from everyone else were Miranda, Victor, and Chris. My gaze faltered at Victor as I approached to claim the empty seat between him and Chris. Like most of the audience, he was glowing. His was a dark red that seemed to coat his skin.

My mouth went dry as I tried to remember our conversations. I'd never asked if he was a regular human. I had just assumed he was. But he had also never mentioned that he wasn't.

What is he? Was he hiding it? Wait... he said he wanted to remember that I was special too. Did he assume I knew? Is it rude to ask? My eyes slid past him to the councilors, who were waiting patiently for me to take my seat.

I took my place next to Victor, forcing myself to sit straight despite every muscle in my body being sore. My muscles screamed at me to slouch for a minute, but I ignored them. I just had to make it through this meeting, and then I could relax. There were too many people, including Travis, Trinity, and Chad from the Wildwood Meadery and a few other people I recognized from around town. I couldn't show anyone how tired I was. Fatigue was weakness. My coven took the seats immediately behind me, Heather pausing to squeeze my shoulder before sitting down.

Steven spread his hands across the table the city councilors sat at and leaned forward. "All right, now that everyone is here, let's begin. We would like to welcome the concerned citizens who have self-identified as preternatural beings. It's always heartening to see community members being involved. However, I would like to remind everyone, although I am sure all of you know this goes without saying, that this is technically a closed session and any talk of what is discussed here today is for admitted guests only. Now, Miss Miller, I understand you identified the suspect."

He sat as I pushed myself to my feet. "I did." I held my head high as I explained what had happened since my last update, ending with my confrontation with John the day before. "I confirmed that his shoe prints matched those I found at the scene and managed to get a confession from him as well." I sat back down a bit more heavily than intended. I hid a wince and draped my hands over my crossed knees to hide any lingering tremors.

Chris stood next. "After we took him in, we got a search warrant for his house, where we located a torn-up land-sale deal. According to Mr. Barfield, Avery backed out of their deal at the last minute. He was attempting to reacquire land his father had sold to her a few years prior. When he went to confront her about it, he saw the volunteer packet for Amanda's campaign and lashed out. He is... arguing self-defense. The prosecutor is not taking that argument seriously."

My eyes bulged. *Self-defense over hurt feelings?*

"And I'm assuming the physical evidence lines up with the confession?" Arthur asked.

Chris took a seat as Victor stood, running his hands over his Regency-era coat and straightening it, then hooked his thumbs into the waist-jacket pockets. "I can confirm that it does. Mr. Barfield's rifle is an exact match for the wound on her head. She appears to have had some sort of wood rot in her head, which made her more susceptible to these sorts of injuries. It's really very unfortunate."

I kept my eyes focused forward as he spoke. My thoughts stuttered over wood rot. *Is that what made her behavior change over the last month? Poor Avery.*

Steven nodded along, his long fingers steepled in front of his face. "Given these facts, it appears the case should be officially transferred to the sheriff's department. With Mr. Barfield not being part of the preternatural community, the local courts would be the best place for him to be tried. Does anyone want to officially put forward that motion?"

Helen raised her hand.

"Seconded," chimed in Arthur.

"All those in favor, say aye."

Everyone at the table responded with a yes.

"And the case is officially transferred," Steven said. "Congratulations, Sheriff Harris."

"Hold on." Miranda straightened in her seat. "Just a note for the record. While I do concede that the culprit turned out to be a normal human, this time, we shouldn't assume that will be the case for crimes against supernaturals—or preternaturals as you like to call them—moving forward. As I've stated before, this really should have been part of my jurisdiction, as the victim was dryad. And honestly, I could have handed the case over to Sheriff Harris at its conclusion, just as easily as Miss Miller did, once I determined who the criminal was."

"Absolutely not." Travis surged to his feet. "If the Wardens had been in control of the investigation, I would have been blamed for it. It's the easy answer. I know how they work."

Miranda smirked at him. "Does that mean you would prefer a regular old human investigating crimes against your pack? Or are you more concerned with pack justice? This isn't the Wild West."

Travis snorted. "No. But after how Megan handled this case, she's proven that she's not going to stop until she gets to the right answer. She should do it."

I snapped my mouth closed.

"She's a liaison," Miranda stuttered. "A farmer. She has no formal training."

Travis shook his head. "I've seen how Wardens run things in other towns. I, for one, would prefer that a local be in charge of these things here instead of some outsider who doesn't understand us."

Trinity and Chad both stood. "We agree."

Dani and Kim stood next, adding their voices to the mix.

My stomach dropped, and my heart skipped a beat as more and more people stood around the room, saying they agreed. I didn't know what I had done to garner so much faith, but they were choosing me over someone who was arguably a lot more qualified. They were choosing me over Miranda.

Edgar's voice cut through the noise. "That's all well and good. This investigation went well. But come on. How serious can she be as an investigator? I can't be the only one who saw her riding around town on the back of a cow."

I gritted my teeth. He could dislike me all he wanted, but Gertie didn't deserve to be mocked like that. I moved to stand, but Chris put his hand on my shoulder and shook his head.

"That's immaterial." Chris stood. Almost the entire room was standing. My eyes tracked between Chris and Edgar as they stared each other down. "I trust her to triage cases when something odd comes up."

"Do we really want someone that unprofessional to represent the town?" Edgar scoffed.

Miranda sighed. "Traveling with a familiar isn't unprofessional. I suppose I can trust her to triage cases as well. For now."

"It's not normal," Edgar argued.

"None of us are normal!" Travis bellowed.

Helen pinched the bridge of her nose. "Edgar, please concede the cow point so we can move on."

"Fine," he bit out.

"Good." Nicholas, the youngest of the councilors, smiled out at the room. His eyes were excited. He spoke with his hands moving in a more animated way than I had seen before. "To me, it looks like we have a mandate from the community. Why not add this to her liaison duties? It's a logical fit."

Steven nodded. "Are you formally putting that motion forward?"

Nicholas looked out over the crowd, his eyes passing from face to face. His gaze finally landed on mine, and his smile warmed. "Yes."

"Seconded," Helen said.

My ears were ringing as Steven called for a vote. The only objector was Edgar. Chris and Victor both agreed to contact me immediately if they came across anything unusual. My mouth went dry as my new reality settled over my shoulders. My role had been changed drastically. This week was a whole new beginning.

The room emptied out behind me as the city councilors began to pack up their belongings.

"Amanda's going to be pleased," Arthur said as they shuffled past. "Now she's running unopposed."

"Great." Helen sighed. "I just hope our meetings don't devolve into conversations about zoning all the time. It's dry, even for me."

Their voices continued down the hallway as I continued to sit there, staring blankly ahead. *How many more of these cases am I going to have? Will it always be this dangerous?*

"Megan?" Victor called from a few feet away.

My head jerked toward him. "Sorry. I... I was just thinking."

"I probably had that exact same facial expression when you left me in the morgue with all those bees. Even after all these years, it's probably the strangest thing I've ever seen."

All these years? How old is he? Does he even age the same way most people do? My mind whirled. I studied him for a second before my thoughts finally snagged on the word *bees.* "Oh gosh, the bees. I forgot to follow up with you about them."

"Don't worry. This lovely lady came by with her husband to pick them up. They weren't stuck in that drawer for long." Victor smiled. "I wanted to let you know I'm looking forward to working with you in the future and was curious if you were still interested in looking over the field guide with me."

"Yeah. I'll probably need to have a crash course now that my job's expanded."

"Friday night? We could do it over dinner. I make a mean carbonara."

My heart skipped a beat, and a flush rose up the sides of my neck. "I would love that." *And maybe then I'll be able to guess what you are.*

He rapped his knuckles against the table and turned to leave. I started to relax into my seat when I noticed I wasn't alone in the room yet. Miranda stood by the door, studying me.

She sauntered over to me, her head held high. "You played your role beautifully."

"What?" My brow furrowed.

"This town was so close to handing over all supernatural investigations to a mundane man. I knew that if I pulled you in, with your enchantment specialty, we would be able to keep in control of it. They can't help but love you, just like they can't help but hate me because of the reputation the Wardens have. We'll be the perfect good cop, bad cop combination."

My heart sank. *Is she right? Are they only choosing me because of my enchantment magic?*

"I'll see you around. Partner." She spun on her heel and stalked out of the room.

I sat there, my mind whirling, for a few minutes after she left. Eventually, I stood and made my way outside. My limbs were heavy, my heart even heavier. *Would Victor be inviting me anywhere if I had a different specialty? How am I supposed to know if people like me for me and not just because of my magic?*

I walked in a daze to the Slice of Life diner, where I had agreed to meet my coven after I got out. Kim and Heather were already in their seats when I got in line behind Dani.

We shuffled forward together.

She bumped me with her elbow. "You doing all right?"

"I... no."

"Anything I can help with?" she asked.

I shrugged.

"Is it the new responsibilities? I know I never had them officially handed to me, but I do have some experience in handling the pressure."

"How did you do it?" I asked.

It was her turn to shrug. "I always stayed curious. And exercised. It takes more cardio than you would think."

"Cardio?"

She gave me a solemn nod, but she had a bit of mischief in her eyes. "From all the running for my life."

I chuckled.

She wrapped her arm around me and squeezed. "You're going to be fantastic."

I stiffened with her arm around me. *Am I in her coven for me or because I somehow made her let me in with magic?* I closed my eyes. *No. She's a divination witch. She would know if I was doing something to her. Our connection is real. This is real. Miranda can't take that away from me. Dani is my friend.*

But no matter how emphatically I told myself that, part of me still rebelled against the idea. I still needed time to process and to figure out if Miranda was right. My mind groped for a change of subject. "Do you know what you're ordering yet?"

"Nope," Dani said.

I cocked my head and studied her. "Why not?"

"I usually let Abby surprise me. She hasn't guessed wrong yet about what meal I'll like."

Dani stepped up to the counter. She bantered with Abby for a few seconds before letting Abby choose for her. Abby's faint glow pulsed as she rattled off an order.

"That sounds perfect," Dani said.

I smiled as I stepped up next. Pride about the magical eye shadow surged inside of me, pushing my negative self-talk to the background. It was a good spell. It let me see all the different varieties of supernaturals in the community. Even those who probably didn't know about it themselves—like Abby, who seemed to have the power to always know the perfect order.

"What will it be?" she asked.

"Surprise me."

Curious to see how what Harriet Spellman's Field Guide looks like? Join our mailing list for exclusive updates and receive a copy of the Dryad field guide entry.

THE NEXT BOOK IN THE SERIES

Ready for the next enchanting adventure? You can pre-order Book 2, 'Murder Between the Stacks,' here.

In book 2, Megan Miller has only been Point Pleasant's supernatural liaison to the notorious Wardens of the West for two months. She thought she'd have more time before facing another murder.

She was wrong.

When a beloved bookstore owner is found dead, Megan is pulled into a supernatural murder investigation that quickly proves more complicated than anything she's handled before. The victim was a vampire, and nothing about the case feels simple. A confession comes too easily. Witnesses choose their words too carefully. And the truth seems tangled in supernatural politics Megan is only beginning to understand.

With her coven at her side and her instincts pushing her forward, Megan must follow the trail wherever it leads—

even if it means stepping deeper into a world that doesn't want its secrets uncovered.

Because in Point Pleasant, immortality doesn't guarantee safety… and every mystery leaves a mark.

Perfect for fans of witchy small towns, found family, and cozy mysteries with a magical twist, this paranormal cozy will have you sitting on the edge of your seat.

ALSO BY ELOISE EVERHART

A Williams Witch Mystery

Potions and the Pleasantly Poisoned

Tomes and the Tangled Trail

Divinations and the Disappearing Dead

Hexes and the Haunted House

Spells and the Suspiciously Silent

Grimoires and the Ghostly Guest

Enchantments and the Eerily Ensnared

Rituals and the Restless Remains

Charms and the Cursed Coven

A Miller's Magical Mystery

Murder Among the Hives

Murder Between the Stacks

ABOUT THE AUTHOR

Eloise Everhart lives in the Pacific Northwest. Her childhood was marked by voracious reading and tabletop roleplaying games, fueling her lifelong passion for storytelling.

By day, she's a dedicated insurance adjuster. It's a career that has honed her sharp eye for detail and developed her inquisitive mind—a skillset she now seamlessly integrates into her cozy mystery writing.

Beyond her storytelling ardor, Eloise is a devoted wife, sharing her home with a menagerie of rescued cats and dogs who have found their furever home in the Everhart household.

ACKNOWLEDGMENTS

I can't believe I'm writing my second series. In starting a new series, I learned that the coming up with a new series arc is just as difficult as the first one. Once again, I have been fortunate to be supported by friends, family, and my wonderful editors. Without their contributions, this book would still be a mess on my hard drive.

To my editors Rashida Breen and Sarah Carleton, you added depth to my story, while helping me cut out the extraneous words that still litter my first drafts even after all these books.

To my beloved husband, Nate, I will never understand how I got to be so lucky to have you in my life. You support me no matter what. Without you, my courage would waver, and I would become lost in the rewrites. To my sister, Andrea, I appreciate your unwavering support. To my father, Chas, and my mother, Tammy, your continued words of encouragement give me strength. I will forever be grateful for your love and support.

I would also like to dedicate this book to my grandmother, Kay. While I was going through the final round of edits on this book, she passed away. She was the inspiration for the spirited Retirees. I will miss you deeply.

And as always, I would like to give a special thanks to someone who is no longer with us, Andrew Henderson. For years you were my writing partner, my confidant, and my greatest friend. I will forever be grateful that you made me start writing again. I will carry your memory with me always.

"Come on a journey with me."

www.ingramcontent.com/pod-product-compliance
Lightning Source LLC
LaVergne TN
LVHW051002080826
845145LV00009B/2416

* 9 7 8 1 9 6 2 7 5 9 0 9 0 *